+   pen marks 4.07   '77 0418'7

THE
290

Also by
SCOTT O'DELL

The Black Pearl
Child of Fire
The Cruise of the Arctic Star
The Dark Canoe
The Hawk That Dare Not Hunt by Day
Island of the Blue Dolphins
Journey to Jericho
The King's Fifth
Sing Down the Moon
The Treasure of Topo-el-Bampo
Zia

THE
290

Scott O'Dell

Houghton Mifflin Company   Boston   1976

This book is for my grandson,
Scott Anderson

Library of Congress Catalog Card Number 76-42097
ISBN 0-395-24737-3

Foreword ⤳

⤳*The name of Raphael Semmes* is known to very few. The reason is not hard to find: history, as often noted, is written by the victors.

Yet from the time of the Romans until the days of World War II, no commander of a galley or a ship or a U-boat, or flight of navy bombers has equalled this man's exploits. He was the greatest raider of them all.

The lives of Semmes and the *290*, which serve as the background for this story, are taken from the history books. The secret building of the *290* at Laird's of Liverpool in the year 1862, her trial run down the Mersey, the efforts of the American Minister, Charles Francis Adams, to seize her as an enemy ship, the counter efforts of James D. Bulloch, the Confederate representative in London, to prevent her seizure are faithfully set down. As are the secret outfitting at the Azores, the mutiny arranged by George Forest, the battle at Cherbourg between the

v

290 and *Kearsarge*, the Federal sloop of war, and the rescue of survivors by the yacht *Deerhound*.

Semmes sailed some ten thousand nautical miles before the battle of Cherbourg. He raided the Azores, the bleak waters of the North Atlantic, the eastern seaboard, and the Caribbean. He even rounded the Cape of Good Hope and hunted Northern ships in the far seas of the Indies, most of the time with the North's best cruisers hot on his heels.

During the long voyage, Captain Semmes captured, burned and sank sixty-nine enemy ships. What's especially memorable is that he did all this without the loss of a single enemy life.

The Author

Chapter ONE

290 was a strange name for a ship. In my two years at Laird and Sons I had never heard one like it. I had helped build the *Jamaica Queen,* the *Black Stingaree,* the *Gosling,* the *Bride of Lahore,* and the *Catamount.* But nothing as odd-sounding as the *290.*

William Bromley, the engineer and architect to whom I was apprenticed, said it was just a temporary name.

"They haven't thought of a good one yet," he said, "so they've just given her a name to tide her over until they can think of something more fitting."

Mr. Bromley was a logical man and this seemed to me a logical thought, so I forgot about the odd name of the ship we were building. And everyone else did, though we all talked about the ship herself.

It was a November night and raving cold, the Liverpool cold that comes in off the sea and up the

1

Mersey and you can't see a foot in any direction, not that there's much to see in Liverpool. Where the cold comes from I don't know, unless it be from Greenland, which is not far away.

We — four friends and I — were in the Mermaid's Grotto, playing a game of darts, minding our own business, when someone sitting behind us with a mug in one hand and a long, pale cheroot in the other made a noise that sounded like "pssst."

I tossed my dart, missed the bull's-eye, which I had needed to win. I turned about, ready to give him a bit of lip for his interruption, when I saw the young man smile in a serious sort of way and with the hand that held the cheroot beckon me to his side.

I had trouble seeing through the haze of cigar smoke, and until I was close up failed to recognize him as my brother, Ted Lynne.

In the six years since I had seen him, he had grown tufts of blond side whiskers and his pink skin had become rosy. This and his fleshy, round face made him look more than ever like our father. Indeed, if he had not grown into Father's image, I wouldn't have recognized him.

He held out a hand. "How are you, Jim? Looking fine, I'd say. Filled out and grown tall."

"How's Father?" I asked, thrusting out my hand.

"Getting older. A little creaky in the joints. Short of temper."

2

I had not seen my father since I was ten, when we stood on the levee in New Orleans and with a wave of his hand he sent me off to England to be educated. I had received letters from him on my birthday, at Christmas, and regular money drafts when I was in school and for the first year of my apprenticeship. Also he had sent promises now and then, through various ship captains, that he was coming to London soon, and we'd have a fine dinner together. I had nearly forgotten him. The truth was, he had nearly forgotten me.

"How is he faring with the war?"

"The war hasn't hurt profits any."

"Does he still have the plantation and warehouse in Haiti?"

"Yes, and he goes back and forth a couple of times a year. I helped him until we had a fight. Lately I've been working on something else. Sit down and I'll tell you about it. There may be something in the deal for you. Money."

The game was over and another had already started. Since I would not be missed, I took a seat across from him. He ordered two mugs of ale and was silent until they came. Then he took a long draw on his cheroot, a swig of ale.

"I hear you're doing well at Laird's," he said.

"Where did you hear it?" I thought he was gulling me. "From whom? Mr. Bromley?"

"No, from other reliable sources. But I'm not surprised. You were always a bright lad and a lover of ships. Even the fat old paddlewheels that came into port. You'd disappear, when you were no more than six or seven, but we'd always know where to find you. Down at the river, staring wide-eyed at the ships, especially the schooners that came in from London or Boston or the Indies."

He paused and took a puff on his cheroot. "I hear Laird's is about to finish a new ship. I hear that she's a long one, but quite narrow in the beam — a good ten feet narrower than usual."

I knew her exact dimensions. She was two hundred and thirty-five feet overall and drew fifteen feet of water. But this was information that neither Laird's nor Mr. Bromley wished to give out. To Mr. Bromley, a ship was very personal. He would as soon give out his wife's dimensions as the figures on one of his ships. But for some reason he was extra close-mouthed about the *290*. As a matter of fact, I myself would not have known her size had I not measured her off with the tape.

Ted ordered two more mugs of ale, but mine I only sipped.

"She's called the *290*," my brother said.

"A temporary name."

"Fortunately," he replied, lighting another cigar,

4

this one long but dark in color. He puffed out smoke that smelled like burning molasses. "Long and narrow, she won't be much of a cargo ship, would you say?"

"I don't know what she'll be," I answered truthfully. "Perhaps she'll be used by the Royal Navy. Their ships are mostly narrow in the beam."

"She's built for speed."

"Possibly."

"Probably." Ted finished off his ale and for moments watched the game that was going on merrily without me. "Can you give me from time to time — say, every other day — a report on when the *290* will make her trial run? It will be worth your trouble."

"My reports would not be worth much. Besides that, it would put me in the position of a spy to report to you what goes on at Laird's."

"Spy? My eye. There's nothing that's secret at Laird's. The ship is even written about in the newspapers. I could walk in the yard tomorrow and speak to Mr. Bromley himself."

"Then why don't you? Why do you need reports from me?"

"As a matter of fact, there are no secrets about her structure. Similar ships have been built before. I simply want to know how things progress. When the

290 will make her trial run down the Mersey."

"Ask Mr. Bromley. He'll know. My reports would not be accurate."

"I'll take that chance. As I've said, it would be worth your while."

"In what way?"

"In pound notes. Twice what you are making in a month."

I had no intention of giving him any information about the *290*. I had done drawings for two ships while I was at Laird's, but nothing of importance. With the *290* I was responsible for designs in the engine room. I worked hard on them in the daytime and dreamed about them at night. The ship was closer to me than my family or friends. She was my whole life.

He could see that this did not impress me, as well he might. He crushed out his cheroot, asked for his cloak, and while putting it on said, "I'll be here tomorrow at the same hour. I'll look for you."

Without further words he went quickly on his way, using a cane with a bright gold head carved in the shape of a lion's claw. His jaunty walk was the same one I remembered from long ago, as if he owned the world — or was about to buy it.

Chapter ~~
TWO

⌇⌇The next evening before I left to play darts at the Mermaid, I thought to ask Mr. Bromley about my brother's interest in the *290*.

"He's curious," I said. "Especially, when she'll make her trial run."

"What did you say? Little, I trust."

"Nothing. I told him to ask you."

"A proper answer."

Ted was already at the Mermaid's Grotto when I arrived, seated off in a private alcove that overlooked the river.

He ordered two drinks, mine of a strong variety, more like a rum punch.

"Does the work progress?" he asked.

"There are slow days and fast days," I said. "This was a fast one."

My brother finished two brandy flips before he asked me if I knew that the *290* was being built by the Southern states as a raider.

I didn't and I told him so. "I've never heard a word about her being built for that purpose."

"England is neutral. Officially she's taken no sides in the War Between the States," Ted explained. "She's even signed a treaty to that effect, but nonetheless the 290 is being built in an English shipyard by English workmen for use as an armed raider to destroy Northern commerce."

"There's no evidence anywhere in the hull that she's being constructed for warfare," I said. "She's heavily built, but there are no special timbers, or reinforcements, or storerooms for powder and shell. I think you're dreaming, Ted."

"If you were building a raider," he said, unmoved by my information, "if you were an architect and someone asked you to design a ship for raiding commerce, what is the first thing you'd do? You'd build her so that she'd sail fast, wouldn't you, Jim?"

"That would be first," I admitted.

"Does the 290 strike you as a hull designed for speed?"

"She's narrow in the beam."

"She's also being fitted to carry sail. Isn't that true?"

"She'll have sails."

"And she'll have powerful engines, too. Sails, narrow beam, and engines. What does that add up to? A cargo ship?"

"A fast cargo ship," I said. "Perhaps."

Ted smoked his cheroot down to a stub and from it lighted another. He offered me one out of a case that looked as if it had been made from crocodile hide.

I thanked him and refused his offer, still remembering my first experience with a cheroot purloined from my father's humidor. My father brought cheroots from Haiti packed in a wicker hamper and smoked them faster than my brother. I did not have my father's talent as a smoker of cheroots, light or dark, made in Haiti, or Cuba, or anywhere.

"You'll grow up to them someday," Ted said sarcastically.

But I was now sixteen and my chances were getting smaller and smaller. Being sick from a cheroot was the only thing worse than being sick from the sea.

"Most of the English have taken up sides on the war in America," my brother said. "Where do you stand?"

"With the South, of course. I've been thinking lately of going home and enlisting in the navy."

"I wouldn't be in a hurry, if I were you. You're too young, Jim."

"How about you? You're twenty-four."

"I tried to join up with the cavalry, but they wouldn't have me on account of my eyes. I see very little. I guess I inherit Father's weakness in that regard."

I doubted that he had tried to enlist, but didn't show my doubt. "How does the war go? I hear a lot of conflicting rumors. One side winning, then the other."

"At the moment, it's a stand-off."

Ted took a long time to knock the ash from his cheroot. "You don't remember much about Father, being so young when you came here. Tell me, Jim, did you know when you were growing up what your father was doing when he was gone from home for months at a time?"

"He traded in sugar. I know because often he brought some of it home."

"When he wasn't hauling sugar, what did he haul?"

"Muscovado, rum, cotton — all the things that ships carry that sail the Indies."

"But do you remember that he owned two ships, the *Santana* and the *Chubasco*?"

"I remember him taking me on one of them. I don't know which it was."

"It would be the *Chubasco*. The big one. A white ketch."

"I don't remember, except once when Father took us to Cuba I was climbing the ladder of the big ship and he grabbed hold of my arm and said I couldn't go aboard because it was carrying sickness. One of the sailors had smallpox. I remember that but little else."

"What's the most profitable of all the cargoes they carry in the Indies?" Ted asked.

"Slaves, I guess."

"You're right, Jim. Slaves from Port-au-Prince to Cienfuegos. To all the plantations in Cuba. By the thousands."

He had ordered a haunch of venison and he was cutting it up into dozens of small pieces. He had done the same thing when he was younger. It bothered me then and it bothered me now.

"Father, as you know, hauled some of those thousands," my brother said. "He rounded up slaves all over Haiti and took them to Cuba. He has a regular barracoon in Port-au-Prince where he keeps them until they are sold." Ted glanced up at me. "He's a slave trader, you know."

"I didn't know."

"You know now."

"Slave trading is illegal," I said.

"Sure, but that doesn't make any difference to your father. He's selling more slaves than he ever did."

"I don't believe it."

My brother shook his head, as if he pitied my ignorance. "Remember the time you wanted to go

11

aboard the *Chubasco*," he explained. "Well, you didn't go on board because your father grabbed you by the arm and said that there was sickness aboard. It wasn't sickness the ship carried. It was several hundred Negroes crammed in the hold. In a space big enough for a hundred. I was there. I saw him grab your arm to keep you off the ship. You remember that well because you've spoken of it. Do you remember the stink that came welling up out of the ship's insides? And you asked Father what the bad smell was and he said it came from the sickness aboard the ship?"

I remembered the smell. I tasted it now as I ate the venison I had ordered. It was on my tongue, in my throat.

I said nothing. I couldn't.

Seeing that I was speechless, my brother went on with his venison, sipping ale and making mournful noises in between, as if the past haunted him.

"I can see, Jim, that you haven't given the war a lot of thought. But why should you, living here in England such a long time. You're more English now than American, judging from your clothes, the way you talk, and the way you think, your whole get-up."

"Underneath, I'm a Southerner."

"You can be one and still not want to fight for slavery."

12

"I haven't thought much about slavery, but I do know that from what I remember and what I've heard here in Liverpool, I am dead set against it."

"Then you should be fighting for the North. You should help get rid of the *Agrippina*. You don't need to do more than you want to, mind you. And think of the money. I guess you could use an extra pound or two."

Chapter ~ THREE

~ *Ted and I* ran into each other the next day at the main gate of the Laird shipyard. It was a bitter cold morning. We would have been comfortable inside the warm pub, not a dozen steps away, but my brother, I presume, did not want to be overheard.

"I trust that the information I revealed last night," he said, "did not upset you too much."

"No, it didn't," I said. I had gotten over my first surprise.

"The wind's cold," my brother said. "Let me tell you why I am here. You've heard of the *Agrippina*?"

"Very little, but I hear she's a tub."

"Not exactly. She's made a dozen voyages to Cuba. But that's not the point."

"What *is* the point?" I asked, feeling the wind through my light coat. Ted was a great one to beat about the bush, if he could find one handy.

"Well, let's start from the beginning. First, the *290* is being built as a raider for the Confederates.

14

According to English law, she can't be built in England as a raider. Therefore, as soon as she makes her trial run the *290* will sail for the Azores. There she'll meet the *Agrippina*. Meanwhile the *Agrippina* is being loaded from keel to gunwales with extra spars, cordage, sails, coal, cannon, shot, powder — everything necessary for the outfitting of a raider."

My mind was wandering. Ted brought it back with a sharp nudge of his elbow. "Do you get the scene?"

I nodded and we moved around the corner, where the wind was less searching. He waited until a group of workers passed out of hearing.

"The *Agrippina*," he said, "is the key to the situation. She's lying now at the East India docks in London. They've been working around the clock on her. She's being stuffed full as a goose with war materials and armament."

He moved closer to me, as if he were about to whisper something. He paused as if he were making up his mind whether to trust me or not. Then he reached out and pinched my cheek in a friendly way, as he used to do when I was a boy, and smiled his winning smile.

"The *Agrippina* will be ready to sail inside of three weeks or a month. My job is to prevent her. To burn her to the waterline."

I was surprised. I didn't think that Ted had tried to enlist, but I did think that he was loyal to the South.

"Here's where you can help. You're to report to me as soon as you learn the hour the *290* is to make her trial run. That information is crucial. You'll hear a day or two beforehand, perhaps sooner. The North has a lot of money to use against the *290*. You can get some of it. Both of us can."

"If the *Agrippina* is the key to the situation," I asked in a practical tone, "then why not destroy her now?"

"If she's destroyed now and the *290* doesn't sail for three weeks, there'll be time for the South to find another ship and gather the bulk of what she'll need."

"As I've told you, I would feel like a spy, giving out reports on the *290*. I have worked on her from the beginning. I have worked hard. I have a part in her. I love the ship."

My brother's face grew pale, as it always did when he was angry. I get red, so I have been told, but Ted always grew pale, his whole face at once.

We stood facing each other. He put his hand on my arm, as if this touch would settle everything, and tried to smile.

"We'll get the report, don't worry," he said, taking

another tack. "With or without your help. My only thought was to give you a chance to make a ten-pounder or two."

Laird's whistle blew a long blast. I always prided myself on being at my drawing board on time, even if I had an excuse for being late. I shook hands with my brother, although I did not feel like doing so, and walked off toward the gate.

It was good to get back into a warm room.

I climbed onto my tall working stool and laid out my drawing with a grateful sigh. We had a good-sized fireplace in the office where I worked with Mr. Bromley and it always burned cheerfully on cold days. Laird and Sons were never ones to pinch on coal, though it was somewhat expensive that year of 1862.

Mr. Bromley's drawing board was at the far side of the room, where he could look out and see at least two of the ships we were working on. One of them was the *290*.

"Have you heard?" he said, but didn't give me a chance to answer. "We're sending her out day after tomorrow. The first thing Wednesday morning."

"That's good news," I answered, deciding to say something about what Ted had just told me.

"And they've changed her name to *Enrica*," Mr. Bromley said. "That's 'Henrietta' in Spanish."

17

Mr. Bromley lit his long-stemmed pipe. He was also long and thin, with a bald head and silver-rimmed glasses that sparkled when the firelight struck them. He was a fine architect and a fine man to work for. I often confided in him and sometimes I thought of him as a father.

"I've just come from another meeting with Ted Lynne," I said. "He's in with a band that's conspiring to burn the *Agrippina*."

"The supply ship for the *290*!"

"Yes. He still is after me for information about when the *290* will sail. I told him I didn't know. And, in so many words, that if I did know I wouldn't tell him."

Mr. Bromley removed the pipe from his mouth and looked at me over the top of his glasses.

"Your brother is from the South, like you. Why is he conspiring against his own part of the country? It's puzzling."

"It puzzles me, too, Mr. Bromley. He's had a fight with our father, who's thrown him out of the house and cut him off from his inheritance. But that hardly seems a good reason for being a turncoat."

"Hardly. There must be something else."

"Well," I said, "he always was greedy about money."

Chapter
FOUR

Within a day of the meeting with my brother, Ted, the newspapers picked up the story of the *290* and carried the news on their front pages.

From these accounts I gathered piece by piece a picture of the events during the past year that I had not known before. I learned about the argument raging between James D. Bulloch, the Confederate representative in London, and the American minister, Charles Francis Adams.

A year or so after I came to work for Laird and Sons, money had been collected in Cuba, Haiti, and places in the South, so the papers said, and sent to England to be used for the Confederate cause.

Soon afterward James Bulloch had arrived in Liverpool and signed a contract to build a ship to be used in commerce. But as time passed, as the *290* took shape, another Confederate raider, the *Sumter*, was making attacks upon Northern commerce.

At this moment, because the building of the *290* was moving along rapidly, things became clearer to Charles Francis Adams and his secret agents. The latter now spent their time in Liverpool, closely watching the progress of the ship and trying to bribe workmen in the shipyard to tell what they knew.

The Northern agents learned much. They learned that the barkentine James Bulloch claimed was being built for commerce was not a commercial barkentine at all. It was to be a fast and deadly Confederate raider.

At this moment, because the *290* might sail any day, the controversy between Adams and Bulloch reached its height.

In the middle of the bitter fight was the British government. Many of its leading men were solidly pro-Confederate. Lord Palmerston, the prime minister, let it be known that he despised the upstart American government, which was not as old as he was. And William Gladstone, chancellor of the exchequer, amused himself, it was said, by redrawing the map of the United States. The House of Commons was pro-Confederate five to one.

Against this powerful anti-Federal opposition, Minister Adams had fought in vain. Now at the hour when the *290* was ready to leave the Mersey, he found himself checkmated in his efforts to have the

20

ship seized by the British government. Lord Russell, the foreign minister, was sympathetic, but declared that until proof was given him that the ship was meant as a commerce raider he could not stop her sailing from English waters.

I heard nothing more of my brother's scheme to destroy the supply ship *Agrippina*. Yet efforts to destroy her were made. Only a careful watch of those who came aboard her and the cargo they brought, as well as of the ship herself, prevented her destruction.

Three days after my talk with Ted, the London papers reported that the Thames River Police had discovered a small launch, carrying two kegs of powder, that had run aground in Plumstead Marshes and, near a farmhouse that bordered the marshes, an abandoned skiff. Also reported were three shots fired by unknown parties, presumably aboard the abandoned launch.

But none of the stories drew any connection between the discovery and the *Agrippina*, though one of the papers suggested that it might be related to the plots against the *290*.

The same newspapers that ran stories of the abandoned launch also reported that the long, bitter fight between James Bulloch and Charles Francis Adams had finally reached a climax.

Mr. Bromley followed these events more closely

21

than I did. One morning he said to me, "Bulloch claims that he's being shadowed by Northern agents. And I heard last night that threats were being made against us, against Laird and Sons. They swear to blow up the *290* where she's docked."

The owners of the shipyard took these threats seriously and posted extra guards around the shipyard and in the yard itself. We all had to wear paper badges to get inside the gates, even Mr. Bromley.

During this time I heard nothing from my brother until the evening before the *290* sailed on what was to be her trial run. I was playing darts at the Mermaid with my four friends when Ted walked in and seated himself at a table where he could watch me.

I had a sure hand for darts and won much more often than I lost. Sometimes I had been guilty of losing on purpose, just to keep our crowd together.

My brother called me over to his table and held out a mug of hot rum. "I didn't know you played so badly," he said. "You must have something on your mind. I hope there's nothing you hold against me. After all, we're brothers, aren't we? The fact that we couldn't get together on the *Agrippina* shouldn't stand between us."

"It doesn't," I said untruthfully, and went back to the game.

Chapter ～〇
FIVE

～ *There was* a bright sun and a brisk breeze the morning the 290 went down the Mersey. Mr. Bromley gave me the day off and took it himself, since we both had had a hand in her building.

Word had passed around on Tuesday that the 290 would not sail until the end of the week, but the day before, on Monday, the twenty-eighth of July, James Bulloch received an urgent message advising him that it would be unsafe to leave her in Liverpool longer than another forty-eight hours.

The note, as I understand it, was signed "A Friend," but the Confederate agent was aware that it came from a member of Lord Russell's staff. He immediately left London for Liverpool and got permission from Laird and Sons to take the 290 out on a trial run within twenty-four hours! The word spread fast.

It became a gala affair. Many London and Liverpool dignitaries were invited for the run, as well as a bevy of pretty ladies, who came dressed in colored crinolines. Mr. Bromley was also invited on the trial and he invited me, introducing me to everyone as his assistant. I felt very important as the beautiful, sleek ship floated gaily down the Mersey, escorted by a tugboat festooned with flags, with a brass band playing martial music.

I was on deck when it happened.

We were within reach of the open estuary, moving along with the gentle current. Mr. Bromley was at a table stacked with bottles of champagne, drinking and chatting with the ladies. There was a main saloon forward and through two windows I could see a number of men seated around a long table.

As I passed the saloon, out of curiosity I looked in at a window and saw one of the men, who was seated at the end of the table, get to his feet. He wore, even though the day was warm, a long gray coat. Abruptly he threw it back, revealing beneath it the gray uniform of a naval officer.

I didn't hear all that he said, though he spoke slowly and in a commanding voice. What I did hear came to me unmistakably. It sent a cold ripple down my back.

Spreading his cloak, with his hands clenched at his waist, he said, "This is a Confederate raider, a sister ship of the Confederate *Sumter*. She is proceeding

24

from here to the Azores. All who wish to go with her, remain seated. Those who choose not to go, please repair to the rail."

There was a sudden commotion in the room — shouts, cries, a Rebel yell, long and drawn-out, like the ones Indians are said to make when they are on the warpath. Men were hitting each other on the back, embracing each other.

I quickly passed on and found my way back to Mr. Bromley, still situated with legs well planted in front of the champagne table. He was talking to a girl with pale cheeks and a pale forehead ringed with curls.

"Did you hear the news?" I broke in.

Mr. Bromley gave me a comic look over the rims of his glasses. "No, what? Did our bottom fall out?"

I didn't have a chance to tell him because now everyone was on deck, shouting, yelling, and talking excitedly. Women were screaming in delight. People were running this way and that. The punch bowl of champagne was suddenly empty and no one came to refill it.

Mr. Bromley was a little unsteady on his feet, though the ship neither pitched nor rolled.

"What's happened?" he asked me. "Did we break a record? What's the fuss?"

I tried to answer him all at once. "Nothing's wrong, Mr. Bromley."

"Where's the man with the punch?"

"He'll be along," I said to calm him. "They've just announced that the 290 is a Confederate raider."

"Hoorah!" he shouted, something that I'd never heard him shout before. "Hoorah!"

I tried to gather my wits. "She's on her way to the Islands of the Azores," I blurted. "Those who want to go with her, may. The captain just said so."

The tug had come up and was tossing alongside, bumping against us. None of the tugmen had the sense to put out bumpers.

"To the Azores? Who wants to go to the Azores? Filthy place, I've heard," Mr. Bromley said.

Men were jumping into the tugboat and holding out their hands to assist the ladies aboard.

Mr. Bromley peered over the side, studying the situation. "Who's the captain down there?" No one answered him.

"Put out some bumpers," he shouted down. "Six, anyway. You're ruining our fine planking."

The tug was now nearly full. There were more on her than on the 290.

"Last call. All ashore. Going ashore," a sailor shouted.

"We'll need ten more men," the mate called from the bridge.

Mr. Bromley glanced down at the tug filled with men anxious to be on shore, then at me.

"Double pay. Prize money," someone shouted. "Adventure. Chance to fight the Yankees."

More bottles of champagne were brought. Mr. Bromley helped himself and poured a glass for me.

"Here's to the 290," he said. "May she sink two hundred and ninety of the enemy."

We drank to her, stem and stern, keel and truck — to the Confederacy.

I threw my empty glass overboard. I watched it strike the water. I looked up at Mr. Bromley, who was watching me.

"I read your thoughts," he said. "You're all excited about going to the Azores. Joining up with the 290 to fight the Yankees."

"It's not so much the fighting," I said. "It's the ship. I love her."

"Sure you do. You worked hard on the 290. But that's no good reason for running after her. Getting your head shot off in the bargain."

"What about my job?" I said, scarcely hearing Mr. Bromley's admonition. "Will it be waiting for me when I get back?"

"Likely, but I can't promise you for certain. Take my advice and stay with Laird's. You'll do more good here than there." He could see that I wasn't listening.

The tug whistled twice; two short sneezes. One of the lines was cast off. I held my breath.

The sky had clouded over and a small sea swept into the Mersey. The 290 began to roll.

"She's a trifle narrow in the beam," I said.

"She'll be better under sail," Mr. Bromley casually observed. "When she gets a little wind in her mainsail, she'll steady up."

He walked to the bulwark and added, "I'll take care of the things in your lodging." With cautious agility he went down the ladder. He waved to me from the deck of the crowded tug. There was a flutter of women's handkerchiefs, cheers from the men, the band struck up a gay tune. Slowly the tug fell astern. The music faded away.

I turned to face the oncoming sea, overcome by the meaning of the step I had taken. The engines of the 290 throbbed steadily beneath my feet, like a great heart beating. My own heart beat with them.

Chapter ~ SIX

⟨⟩ *There are* three island groups in the Azores, which are some eight hundred miles off the coast of Portugal.

It is an enchanting group of islands, with deep blue waters lying between them, alive with whales and dolphins. The islands themselves have steep cliffs but higher up there is tillable land, all of it terraced and green, with white houses, red roofs, and orange trees.

Of the islands, Terceira was the best located for the ship's purposes and here, some six weeks after our leaving Liverpool, we anchored. Captain Semmes came aboard the same afternoon.

To my surprise, for I had learned that he had a reputation as a very strict captain, Semmes was a small man, with the trim, elegant look of a Frenchman and a mustache that had long pointed ends. Since he chose to pretend that the *290* was a commerce ship, Semmes respected the Portuguese customs laws and moved the ship a marine league off-shore.

Here we met the *Agrippina* and by Saturday afternoon, three days later, the *290* was shipshape. Shot racks were filled, shell and powder stored, guns mounted, coal bunkers replenished. The old *Agrippina* made ready to leave, to take on supplies the raider would need at a future time. Her first mission was to load a cargo of Cardiff coal and meet the *290* at Martinique in November — without fail.

The following day, a cloudless Sunday, Semmes called all of us on deck, read his commission as captain, and christened the ship the Confederate raider *Alabama*, in honor of his native state. (He always called her by that name, but those of us who came from Liverpool called her the *290*.) A gun went off at the bow, the band struck up a tune called *Dixie*, the Union Jack came down, and the stars and bars of the South was raised.

Then began the long ordeal of signing on. Captain Semmes brought with him a regular crew of officers and men. But there were many aboard who had been shanghaied, seized while they were drunk.

The paymaster came forward with the shipping list, placed it on the capstan, and gave out word that all who wished to enlist should make it known at once. We all drew close to listen. There were

Dutch, English, Welsh, Irish, French, Italian, Spanish, and one Russian — some ninety-odd in all, swept up from the alleys of Liverpool.

"You are all released from the contracts under which you sailed to the Azores," he said. "Should you not wish to enlist, you'll be given free passage home in the *Agrippina* and pay until you reach Liverpool."

His gaze ran over our raggle-taggle crew. It fastened upon me. I was the youngest by far. I could feel my knees shake under me and my mouth go dry. What if he deemed me too young, too frail for the rigors of war? What if I had to step out in front of everyone and make my way down the ladder to the waiting longboat, to be taken to the *Agrippina* and back to Liverpool? Only then, as his gaze rested heavily upon me, did I realize how much I wanted to go with the *290*, the ship I loved, to wage war with her against the North.

The paymaster's gaze stayed fixed upon me. In embarrassment I looked away. Nearby, standing erect against the bulwark, I saw a young Negro, younger than I was, a boy. I squared my shoulders and felt better. The paymaster's gaze moved on.

When my turn came I stepped forward quickly.

"What have you done at sea?" the paymaster asked.

"Nothing, sir, on the sea. But I helped with the design of this ship."

The paymaster gave me an odd look as if he had suspicions about my truthfulness.

"As an apprentice in Mr. Bromley's office," I hastily added.

He straightened the paper in front of him and dipped his pen.

"We'll put you down for the time being as a sailor second class."

"Thank you, sir," I said. "I'll not disappoint you."

"You had better not," the paymaster said, not looking up.

He dipped his pen once more. "What nationality?"

"I was born in New Orleans," I said. "My father is an American."

"Lynne, New Orleans," the paymaster said. He glanced up at me. "Does he have a partner by the name of Cicérone?"

"Yes, sir."

"Does he own two ships, the *Chubasco* and the *Santana*?"

"Yes, sir."

The paymaster said something under his breath and drew a line beneath "sailor second class." Then he called for me to raise my right hand and swear allegiance to the Confederate Navy, which I did. Then he waved me on.

We were promptly issued sailors' gear, fed, and put to work. I was sent to the engine room and given a shovel.

That night I was too excited to sleep. Fortunately I was only in my bunk four hours when I was routed out and sent back to the engine room.

Chapter ⁓
SEVEN

⁓*The whaling season* had reached its height in the Azores. Northern ships, whalers from New Bedford and Salem and Boston, crammed to the gunwales with oil, were making ready for the long voyage home — Captain Semmes chose to remain quietly in their midst. The Portuguese, who owned the Azores, did not know that he commanded a raider. Nor did the enemy's whalers. We flew the flag of France.

The *290* had arrived at the islands with its decks grimed with rubbish. But within a week they were sweet and clean, awnings snugly spread, yards squared to the inch, the rigging hauled tight, all brass ashine. And the men themselves were no longer a gang of derelicts but a crew smartly dressed and anxious to fight.

This was the work of Captain Semmes. At first glance, as I have said, he might have been a Frenchman, with his trim shape, his huge mustache with pointed ends that he carefully waxed every morning and evening and wore a little net over at night — a man you might see at a Parisian café sipping cognac.

But this was a very false impression. Semmes was tough. He gave a command once and expected it to be obeyed on the double. If not, the culprit would find himself on reduced rations or in double leg chains in the forepeak. There was little backtalk, little grumbling, and no shirking of tasks.

The 290's officers, for the most part, Captain Semmes had brought with him from the Sumter and a lighthouse tender he had once commanded. They were disciplined, loyal, and eager.

As for myself, my position began at the bottom of the ladder, or near it, in the coal bunker, but before we left the Azores I was promoted a rung to the task of a part-time wiper in the engine room and, at the evening mess, a mess boy charged with setting table for the officers and cleaning up the debris when it was finished. Lem Wilson, who was two years younger than I, was the official mess boy.

A surprising thing happened to the young Negro before we sailed. Captain Semmes freed him, officially made him a free man, in theory as good as anyone. Lem thought he was free and good as anyone. The event pleased me.

35

Captain Semmes planned everything well. We had met the *Agrippina* at the Azores because the islands were secluded, far distant from the paths of the Northern raiders. Also because, as I have noted earlier, it was the prime hour to seize the Northern whalers, overflowing with their summer catches.

Perhaps now I should describe the *290*. Knowing her so well, it is pardonable that I have not mentioned before how she was put together. The design was novel — suited to her mission and, as I have said, much the work of Mr. Bromley.

She was a single-screw steamer, with long, raking lower masts of yellow pine, a fiddle cutwater, standing rig of the best Swedish iron, an elliptic stern, and full sail power. Two hundred and thirty-five feet over all, she displaced little more than a thousand tons. Two horizontal engines gave her 300 horse-power, though they could deliver more than 1000 when called upon. She drew fifteen feet of water and carried 375 tons of coal in her bunkers, which was fuel for eighteen days of moderate speed. Also she was equipped with a novel two-bladed screw that could be raised into a position well free of the water, and consequently was no drag on her speed when she was under sail.

To give a better picture of a vital part of the *290*, may I say that her main deck was now pierced for a dozen guns, though she carried but eight. Of the eight, six were 32-pounders, three each on port and starboard and two pivots on the center line. At the forecastle, a very strategic location, was a 7-inch Blakely pivot rifle that could fire a 100-pound shot more than four thousand yards. The other Blakely, an 8-inch set up abaft the mainmast, we seldom used. Seen from a short distance, her raking masts and sleek block hull were exciting to behold.

On September 5, 1862, flying the Stars and Stripes, we ran down the *Ocmulgee*, our first captive, a large schooner out of Edgartown, Massachusetts. Lashed alongside her was an immense sperm whale. Her crew swarmed over it, stripping blubber by the yard, when Prize Master Fullam shouted down from the deck of our boarding cutter: "You are a prize of the Confederate States Steamer *Alabama*, Captain Semmes commanding. Fetch your papers and come with us."

The Yankee skipper was at once surrounded by his crew, brandishing their flensing knives, but he saw our pivot rifle bearing full upon him and meekly jumped aboard the cutter. Only then did the Stars and Stripes come down and the Stars and Bars go aloft. It was a ruse we often used. Semmes owned a flag from every country and in time it became a part of my job to keep them in good condition.

Captain Semmes wisely decided not to burn the *Ocmulgee* until the next morning, in fear that if he destroyed her at night it would scare off the large whaling flotilla that was still lying peacefully near at hand.

At dawn her cabin and forecastle bunks were cut open. Straw from the mattresses was mixed with a barrel of lard from the kitchen. Two piles of this mixture were made, one in the cabin and the other in the forecastle. Four men set them afire and before they were back aboard the *290*, the whaler was ablaze.

Black smoke rose in a cloud against the dark mountains of Pico and Fayal as we steamed away. The *Ocmulgee* and her crew, crammed into her cutter, set off for the nearest land, not far distant, helplessly brandishing knives at us.

We captured our second prize within hours. She was the *Starlight*, out of Boston. Three women aboard, bound for Fayal, caused Captain Semmes a problem, but he sent them on their way the next morning. With the rest of the crew, they were put ashore at Pico and the whaler set afire.

We made an eleven-day sweep around the Azores, visiting every likely harbor and inlet, seized eleven ships, all brimming with oil, and burned ten of them. They darkened the skies with oily smoke.

We were in full swing now, with good weather, good hunting, a trim, tight ship, and a happy crew. Except for one seaman, a bull-necked ruffian named George Forest.

Sumter, the smaller raider, which Captain Semmes commanded two years earlier, had caused much damage to the Northern navy until she was sunk. Forest was a seaman aboard this ship but for some reason had deserted.

When we captured the *Dunkirk* a few weeks after leaving the Azores, George Forest was there aboard her, now a seaman fighting for the North. Semmes was surprised — I think outraged — to encounter him again and immediately had him tried and court-martialed.

There then took place the strangest event of my entire enlistment. Even though he had been found guilty, Semmes signed him on as a sailor aboard the *290*. It is true that we were short of experienced hands. It may be that Semmes planned to make Forest pay for his desertion of the *Sumter*.

Whatever the reason, it was still an unfortunate decision, for George Forest proved himself a dangerous troublemaker.

I disliked his looks the moment we ran into each other, the second day he was aboard. He also disliked me, for no other reason possibly than that I disliked him. Our encounter took place at mess, while I was emptying leftovers from my plate.

"Being skinny as a mastpole," he said, watching me scrape off what I hadn't eaten into the mess bucket, "seems to me you'd not throw good food away."

"I happen not to like cabbage," I said. "Nor leeks."

"What does the little lad like?"

"Most everything except cabbage and leeks."

Forrest was broad of shoulder, with a neck that came up in a straight line and joined a chin as sturdy as a mallet. He had pale hair that hung to his chest and small, mean-looking eyes of an indeterminate color.

"There's a funny sound to your words," he said, brushing me aside on his way to the deck. "What are you, a bloody Englishman?"

"Neither bloody nor an Englishman," I answered.

He paused in the doorway and glanced back over his shoulder, squinting his eyes at me. His mouth opened and closed, without a word. Though he said nothing more, I did not look forward to seeing him again.

Chapter ~◇~
EIGHT

~◇~ *In a quiet cove* at the island of Fayal, we spent two days recaulking the upper planking, which had been laid down in an English winter and had begun to gape under the hot sun.

Near the ship dolphins were at play, swimming under our keel, racing off only to dash back and make circles around us again. Two whales that the Yankees hadn't killed sent up plumes of spray on the near horizon.

Between caulking we had drills with the big guns, exercises with pistol and cutlass. Armed with long pikes, we were also taught the art of repelling boarders.

It was a shipshape crew, except for George Forest, and a well-found ship that weighed anchor after the two days. The whaling season was over, the winter storms were coming on.

We left the Azores empty of ships and headed

northwest in the face of a fierce September gale. I looked forward with excitement to Captain Semmes's next exploit. The sea was in my blood and my restricted life aboard ship did not dilute it. The food was good. I got along well with Lem Wilson, the former slave.

One night while we were sitting on the deck in the starlight he asked me about slavery in England.

"We don't have slavery in England."

At first glance Lem looked frail, but he was wiry and tireless. His eyes had a lazy look yet they missed nothing.

"Why's there no slavery in England?" he said.

I answered his question as well as I could. Then I said, "We have a lot of slave dealers in England. I've seen some of them. They bring their ships to Laird's in Liverpool for repair. They're all rich men."

"That's not a good way to get rich."

"It's the worst way I can think of."

"Do you think it's right, me fighting for the South?"

"You're not fighting for slavery, Lem."

"I'm fighting for Captain Semmes. What he says, I do. Where do you think he's going to take us now?"

"Where there are a lot of ships to sink."

Semmes, it turned out, was bound for the Grand Banks and the Eastern seaboard of America.

Strategy he always kept to himself. No one knew

his plans, except now and then his second in command, Lieutenant Kell. He said little and stayed to himself, mostly in his cabin, reading and planning his next foray. Even his navigation officer, Lieutenant Sinclair, could only guess from day to day what his destination might be.

The Grand Banks of Newfoundland was a fresh hunting ground for the *290*. The huge Northern commerce fleet, filled with the rich harvests of the Middle West, took this path on their way to the markets in Europe.

On October 23 of a bright morning the lookout spied two freighters heading straight for us. Captain Semmes kept his course until the two huge ships came nearly abreast, only a few hundred yards away, then wheeled, fired our bow gun, and the Confederate banner, kept clean and well pressed by me, rose to the peak.

The ships were the *Emily Farnum* and the *Brilliant*, both from New York, bound east with cargoes of grain. Semmes burned the *Brilliant* and transferred fifty of his prisoners to the *Emily Farnum* and ransomed her, with the agreement that she would sail to Liverpool.

But the *Emily Farnum* broke her agreement, unbeknown to us, and returned to Boston, where she spread word that our raider was off the coast. Newspapers picked up the news and, though we were not aware of it, the alarm spread fast. It hampered our movements. Yet within twelve days Semmes overtook and burned eight more enemy ships, taking their crews aboard and releasing them at the first port we entered.

As we moved south along the American coast, from the captured prizes we gained valuable reports of ship movements. Aboard the ships Semmes found the *New York Times*, the *Herald*, the *Shipping Gazette*, and other papers. Each of them gave detailed accounts of movements of Northern ships.

It was of great help to Captain Semmes. For one thing, we learned that more than thirty warships were on our trail, as well as their location and the nature of their armament. From this list, Semmes saw that the North had thirteen fighting ships he must avoid at all costs, since they were much larger than the *290* and more heavily armed.

He was tempted, according to a rumor that ran through our ship, to steam through and attack the shipping in New York Harbor. Instead, he gave up this bold gamble and set off for Martinique to rendezvous with the *Agrippina*. We moved cautiously. Not only did we know the number of Northern ships that were trailing us, but also that each had a picture of the *290*, a copy of a photograph taken by someone with a camera before we sailed from Liverpool. She was described officially as looking like "a black swordfish cutting through the seas."

Slipping out of the Gulf Stream, we skirted the regular shipping lanes, but by chance on November 2 we overhauled the New Bedford whaler *Levi Starbuck.*

She proved to be a magnificent warehouse, packed fore and aft with stores for a thirty-month cruise in the Pacific. From her Semmes took New Bedford and Boston newspapers, only four days old, with more important news of Northern ship movements.

But more important still, we rifled from her ample cupboards mounds of fresh vegetables — melons, turnips, cabbages, and rutabagas. It was a welcome haul, for we were threatened with scurvy, having been seventy days on a salt diet.

Semmes burned the *Levi Starbuck*, prize number twenty-two, took her crew aboard, and skirted Bermuda. We kept a night watch for ships returning from eastern seas.

One of Captain Semmes's habits, if it can be called that, was the collecting of flags from the ships he had burned and likewise their chronometers. This foible gave me more work to do. By the time we approached Bermuda waters he had a large collection of both. Something about the cut of my jib or my work in the engine room appealed to him, and he gave me the task of winding his shelf-full of chronometers.

45

This task was larger than it sounds and took much of my leisure time — my regular hours were still being spent at mess and in the engine room. I also kept in careful order the flags of many nations, ready for any emergency, although we commonly used the English Union Jack and the French Tricolor.

About this time, I asked Lieutenant Kell if I might put in an hour each day at the helm. We had two helms, interchangeable and triced. To be on deck, whatever the weather, to feel the motion of the ship through my hands and thus feel the surge and life of the sea itself, was a great pleasure.

It was an unusual request, and Lieutenant Kell took his time to think about it. I then told him that I had been an apprentice to Mr. Bromley, who had helped to build the 290. This tipped the scales in my favor.

From then on, day or night, whenever I had a chance, even if it were only for a few minutes, I stood beside the helsman. Sometimes he gave over the helm. It was then I thought about Mr. Bromley and wished that he was there to see me.

I did write Mr. Bromley a long letter, telling him how fine the ship was and how I was learning to handle the helm that he had spent many hours designing. I mailed the letter from Martinique, but, I was to learn, it never reached him.

Chapter ❧
NINE

☙ *On the eighteenth of November* we were running breezily down the pretty coast of Martinique, having doubled the eastern point of Dominica, when the mutiny took place.

George Forest had a close friend, by the name of Gill, who was always in some sort of petty trouble. Between them they cleverly argued with certain members of their watches, saying that since the *290* had never entered a Southern port, she was commissioned illegally. Seizure of the ship, therefore, would not be mutiny. In any event, mutiny would be easy, Gill said. Indeed, he and three others had mutinied on a Spanish ship, killed her officers, and looted her of a sack filled with silver.

That night, after we had moored at Trinidad, Forest and Gill and those they had persuaded to join them put their plans into action.

In the darkness, Forest slid down the cable, eluding lookouts on deck, and swam to a waiting bumboat, from which he returned with a quantity of fiery Martinique rum. He passed it around among his followers until most of it had been consumed. Thereupon an uproar started on deck, and lights were lit, against orders.

Of a sudden, thoroughly soaked with rum, the whole watch stampeded for the main deck. A boatswain who was so foolhardy as to throw himself in their way was knocked unconscious with a belaying pin.

I was in the engine room when I heard pandemonium overhead. Grabbing a heavy spanner from the workbench, I rushed on deck, not knowing what to expect. The spectacle stunned me.

The watch were running about the deck, waving their arms and shouting threats. They seemed to be marching in a serpentine behind George Forest, who kept shouting, "Mutiny! Mutiny! Come on, let's take the ship!" By his side was Gill.

As I reached the deck and quickly surveyed the scene, I ducked in behind the wheelhouse, aware that my chances were small against a dozen drunken sailors.

At the same moment Lieutenant Kell appeared on deck with a band of officers and petty officers. He ordered that part of the crew who were sober and standing apart from the general melee to seize their drunken shipmates.

There must have been a dozen men in the sober group, but to a man they shouted "No!" to Kell's command and began to edge themselves into Forest's serpentine.

The serpentine had made one drunken round of the deck, passing where I stood against the wheel-house, when Forest's bleary eyes fell upon me. Quickly he slipped out of line and lurched in my direction.

I was within reach of his fists when I lifted the heavy spanner from where it was hidden behind me and brought it down upon his head. The blow glanced off or it would have killed him. As it was, he lay quite still at my feet, spread-eagled upon the deck.

The serpentine stopped; the men milled around for a moment in confusion, staring about for their fallen leader. Then Gill, even larger than Forest, took his friend's place, and everyone began to edge toward me.

My instinct was to dart below for a weapon of some sort. Then I remembered that everything — pistols, rifles, cutlasses — was in the arms chest, under lock and key.

The rioters moved closer. Knives came out of

their sheaths. Some of the men were using sling-shots. They came slowly, aware, perhaps, that below deck there were thirty officers, by now with arms. Forest still lay quiet, but Gill was urging the rioters forward.

About this time, as I stood with my back against the wheelhouse, the spanner clutched in both hands, Captain Semmes appeared. At his waist hung a huge navy pistol. There was a long silence. Some of the rioters began to move back, though Gill still urged them on.

"Mr. Kell," Semmes shouted, "give the order to beat to quarters!"

The fife and drum came up the companionway. The beat of the drum and the shrilling of the fife brought silence. The silence grew deeper. Then the rioters began to move. They moved in an ungainly dash for their gun positions, so ingrained from hours of drill was the call of the "beat to quarters."

Captain Semmes, with a well-armed band of officers, strolled along each gun crew, and seized and ironed on the spot all who were drunk.

Forest had now come to and stood looking around for me, shouting, as he picked up a knife, "Where's that limey lad? I got something for him."

It took five stalwart men to put him in irons.

Twice more Semmes made the rounds of the gun crews, weeding out the last of the offenders. The mutineers were then hauled away to the gangway. The quartermasters let down draw buckets and began to douse the noisiest of the drunks with cold sea water.

The mutineers were mostly foreigners, unused to this form of punishment. They received it with laughter and catcalls.

"Come on, you bloody quartermasters. We're not afraid of water."

Their request was promptly met.

Buckets of water came up faster and faster, in a steady stream, and were dashed in their faces. They began to gasp, then to shiver, and finally fell to their knees, pleading with Semmes not to kill them.

"Captain, are you trying to drown us? For God's sake, Captain. Never will we do it again."

The ceremony took more than two hours. While the rest of us stood by and watched, the mutineers gave up, one by one.

As the last one yielded, Semmes said, "Mr. Kell, give the word to retreat." He ordered their chains removed, and to the music of fife and drums they were sent below to sleep off their drunks.

But George Forest, still glancing around for me, remained defiant. He was placed in double irons until the next day. Then, defiant as ever, he was triced to the mainmast rigging, two hours up and two hours off. The next day he was put ashore. To my great relief, we never saw him again.

Chapter ∼ൟ
TEN

∼ൟ *Our second prize* that week was the small brig
Dauphine, out of Boston.

From our first prize we had picked up sixty-six passengers. Our ship by now was very overcrowded, so
Captain Semmes put all our newly acquired passengers aboard the *Dauphine* and sent her off to Port-au-
Prince.

It was a gallant gesture on his part, since the passengers were on their way home to Haiti when their
ship was captured.

As soon as I heard that the *Dauphine* was to be
sent to Port-au-Prince, I was determined to go with
her. My brother had told me about the barracoon
my father and his partner owned in that city, the
warehouse in which they kept the men, women, and
children the slave catchers caught in the surrounding
hills. Getting up my nerve, I forthwith went to see
Lieutenant Kell.

I located him in his cabin, smoking an unlit pipe and reading a ten-day-old copy of the *Shipping Gazette,* which we had found on the *Dauphine.* He was chortling over the information it gave about the Northern warships, chiefly their whereabouts.

"Lieutenant Kell," I said, "I'm here to ask a favor."

He glanced up as if to gauge how great a favor I was about to ask.

"It has to do with the *Dauphine,*" I said. "As you know, Captain Semmes is sending her with sixty-six passengers to Port-au-Prince. I would like to go along as a member of the crew. I'm a good steersman, something I've learned while on this ship, and I can help out in the engine room, for which I'm qualified."

Somewhat surprised by my request, he took several moments to digest it. Then he said, "It will be a small crew, since we can't spare a large one. Your chances are not good. But I'll give thought to it."

The next morning he stopped me on deck and said that the *Dauphine* was sailing that afternoon. "You'll be going along as a seaman in the engine room. The ship has rusty boilers and a balky steering gear, so be careful and don't blow her up. But why, I'm wondering, do you want to go?"

The truth was I could not give him a straight answer as to why I wanted to go to Port-au-Prince, in a leaky tub of a ship, through dangerous waters no one in our small crew had ever traveled before. It had something to do with seeing the island where my father grew rich. And for some reason I had a desire to meet Ruiz Cicérone, his French partner. Dimly in my thoughts was the barracoon that my brother had spoken about and some wild idea I had about it. But the thoughts were vague and confused. I cannot put them down, even now.

"I've never seen Port-au-Prince," I answered. "And it's exciting to me to have a chance to carry out Captain Semmes's orders, even in a leaky tub with rusty boilers."

"As good a reason as any," Lieutenant Kell replied, unconvinced, I judged by his tone.

The sixty-six passengers were mostly French planters and their wives. I saw them only as they got on the *Dauphine* and as they got off, a fashionable group who had been in New Orleans for some sort of celebration.

The ship was in command of Chief Petty Officer Carroll. He was a young man I knew only slightly, an alert and knowledgeable seaman. He had only five in his crew, but the *Dauphine* was a small brig, not more than a hundred tons, and our docile passengers were very anxious to get home. With favorable winds we made better time than expected.

Our instructions from Captain Semmes were to put the passengers ashore in Port-au-Prince, coal and provision the ship, and return at once to a rendezvous in Cuba. If the *290* was not there when we returned, we were to unload her coal and supplies at Legria, a secluded island, cache everything that could be of use, including the ship's French flag and her chronometer, and meet Semmes at Fayal.

It was a clear evening when we passed the island of Gonave and followed the long blue lizard's tongue of land into Port-au-Prince.

Our excited passengers, who had given up ever seeing their homeland again, were packed and ready to step on the dock long before we tied up. When the ship was clear, Carroll had her moved a half-mile offshore and anchored fore and aft. Then he gave us instructions.

"We'll set a two-man watch and three can go ashore. You can decide or I'll make the choice."

The five of us could not agree, so after some debate Carroll made up the list, sending me ashore with two companions, one of them being Lem Wilson.

Far to the west, as I stood at the rail, the sea darkened and disappeared above the blue sea of the orange groves. At the foot of the mountain the lights of the city began to pick out fluttering shapes in the dusk. A light wind that smelled of orange trees was moving about.

It was no random shape the lamps and the flambeaux slowly built up there below me, but a long, curved saber with its point resting in the jungle, its handle a half-mile away on the shore.

Through my glasses, I followed the twist of the shoreline, the curve of the saber, until I saw the sign, close upon the place where the loading dock came to an end. I knew it was there. My brother had told me its whereabouts.

It was a small sign, but written large: CICÉRONE AND LYNNE. The letters looked to be carved, edged with gilt that had faded. The building was immense but had a dilapidated, forsaken look about it.

I went below and changed my clothes. In less than an hour, with a navy pistol on my hip and no sign about me that I was a seaman, I set off with the others in our longboat. I told Lem, who rowed us ashore, that I would find a boat to bring me back to the *Dauphine* sometime before midnight. Alone, I walked past the warehouse with its faded gilt sign, CICÉRONE AND LYNNE.

A lantern in an iron cage hung over the main doorway and gave off a flickering light. From somewhere in the vast barracoon came the sound of a baby crying, the voice of a girl singing. When the voices had ceased for a moment, I heard a low humming sound, like waves sliding up a faraway beach — the sound of

57

many people moaning. I came to a halt. I stared at the sign, at my father's name in gilt letters. Suddenly I thought about the time long ago when he had stopped me from going aboard the *Chubasco*, the big white ship that my brother said was crammed with slaves.

The moaning ceased. There was a long period of quiet. The moaning began again and there came the faint words of a French song. The song ended and the barracoon was silent once more, so silent that it might have been empty.

Night was fast coming on, but I did not move from where I stood. I continued to stare at the faded sign over the warehouse door. My brother had told me that Cicérone and Lynne employed slave catchers to roam the Haitian countryside, round up parcels of blacks, and cart them here to the warehouse, from whence they were shipped off to Cuba.

It was stifling hot. I opened the throat of my shirt. My head was reeling, but somewhere in my confused thoughts a plan took shape. The plan was shadowy at first, yet as I walked away from the barracoon its outlines became clear. I hurried toward the broad boulevard, which I could see in the distance. At last, realizing that there was little time left to me, I broke into a trot.

Chapter ~
ELEVEN

~ *Boarding* a one-horse calèche I found after a short walk, I asked its driver to take me up the Champs de Mars.

"To where on the boulevard?" the driver replied in English that was good enough for me to understand.

"Anywhere," I answered in English lightly tinged with the Southern accent that I had never lost. "Along the boulevard."

"You are out for the air, Monsieur?"

"Yes, if you can find some." I said. "But for other reasons, too."

The breeze had died. Humid and heavy with the day's accumulated odors, the air had closed in upon me, until it was hard to breathe.

The first stretch of the Champs de Mars was deserted except for a pack of scavenging dogs trotting noiselessly along in front of the carriage, and two shadowy figures propped against a wall.

"There is no one around," I said to the driver.

"Holiday today," he said. "Parties, fêtes everywhere, Monsieur. In the hills where the cool is."

"Take me to the hills," I said. Then I asked his name.

"Thiot, sir. Armand Thiot."

A very aristocratic name, I thought to myself, for the driver of a one-horse calèche.

"The fêtes are in the hills?" I asked.

"*Si*, where the *ricos* are," he replied, suddenly switching to Spanish, which I knew better than French. "Where the cool *vientos* are."

"But where are the poor people?" I asked. "I see only two in half a mile."

"They are beyond. Up toward the hills where it is cool."

"They celebrate there near the hills?"

"*Si*, but not *in* the hills. Below the hills."

I had heard from my father many tales of Port-au-Prince. He told them to me in the evenings after dinner, when he smoked his long black cheroots and spit, as accurate as a rifle shot, into a brass spittoon two strides from where he sat in his stiff-backed chair. They were told to me as other children were told fairy tales.

*

Deserted streets meant that there was trouble in the city.

In Port-au-Prince trouble was chronic, like the fever and smallpox. It came up with the swiftness of a tropical storm. The overthrow of Emperor Faustin some years before had ended the reign of the last of the Negro potentates, but it had only increased anxiety and bloodshed throughout the island.

"No trouble here now?" I asked Armand.

"Well, a little," he said.

I was sure that he was lying. The deserted streets, the empty boulevard, the darkened windows, and the barricaded stores meant only one thing.

"Take me to the home of Ruiz Cicérone," I said. "I don't know where it is, but it may be in the hills."

"I know," said Armand. "He is a man of much money. Very rich. A *rico.*"

The flower-covered entrance in the wall that surrounded the château of Ruiz Cicérone, my father's partner, was closed. Only at the second summons from Armand and the smart crack of his whip did its guardian open the iron gates.

I paid the fare and in addition gave Thiot a handful of silver for his promise to meet me, without fail, at eleven-thirty, the first step in the plan that was slowly forming itself.

"At eleven and a half," he said. "Near the gate. Before that time if you wish, Monsieur."

"I may wish," I said.

Inside, all was in bright contrast to the deserted streets. Dolphins spouted golden fire. The spacious belvederes of the garden were alive with music and voices. There were couples moving everywhere under the trees along glimmering white coral paths.

At the door I asked for Ruiz Cicérone, and when he came out on the broad terrace I introduced myself as James Lynne, the son of his partner, Matthew Lynne.

The light was not good where we stood, but I was sure that his first impression was one of surprise. He knew of my existence, but I doubt that he ever expected to see me standing on the terrace of his home, a grown man, almost.

There was a brief silence after the introduction and he had asked after the health of my father and my brother, Theodore.

"I just came along the Champs de Mars," I said, speaking in French. "I noticed that it's deserted."

"We've had trouble today," he replied. "Something this afternoon about a cockfight. Nothing serious."

Ruiz Cicérone was small, spindle-shanked, and narrow of shoulder, with a head too large for his body, dressed in mouse-colored clothes.

"Papa Rouge, a black troublemaker, is at the far end of the island," Cicérone said. "He was two days ago at Cap Françoise. As long as he's at the Cap, there's no cause for alarm."

My thought was to inquire about Papa Rouge, of whom I had never heard. Instead I asked about news of the war, as he had heard it, and told him that I was a member of the 290's, the *Alabama's*, crew.

His attitude changed suddenly, for whatever reason. He poured me a glass of wine from a festive board nearby and, while I was sipping it, spoke of the damage the raider had done to Northern ships, to shipping in general.

"Your raider has everyone scared out of his wits," he said. "It's practically impossible to find anyone wishing to undertake even the short voyage to Cuba."

"My father mentioned you in a letter I got from him last year. He said that business was not good on account of the war."

"Because of the war and Papa Rouge. It's not so easy anymore to round up a cargo."

Cicérone assumed that I knew about the business, that the sugar and cotton warehouse was only a front for slave-trading.

"And the fact that slavery is now illegal in Haiti," I said.

"That too. My catchers came in last week with only thirty-one, after a month in the mountains. And a very poor crop it is."

"How many do you have on hand?" I asked.

"I don't keep a daily count. The last figure I heard was about two hundred men and women, thirty children of all ages. We haven't been able to ship for more than two months. They're fast eating us out of a profit."

"Perhaps I can help you," I said. "I have a ship that can be used for a trip to Cuba. Or on any short run."

Cicérone put a hand on my arm. "It sounds possible. We can talk about it. By the way, where did you learn your French? You speak it well."

"In New Orleans and at school in England. I speak some Spanish also," I bragged, already light in the head from my glass of champagne.

We were silent. The white gravel clinked underfoot as we strolled among the trees.

"What a pleasant surprise!" Ruiz Cicérone said to make conversation. "But what sends you here?"

I explained that I had brought a shipload of his countrymen, captives of the 290, to the harbor that afternoon.

"We have an empty ship," I said. "We can take all the slaves in the barracoon and land them safely in

64

Cuba. Safely because I know where the *290* is."

I got the impression that he had become wary and uncomfortable with slave-trading.

"My foreman, Apollo, will be at the warehouse," he said. "Apollo knows much more about the cargo than I do. To be frank with you, of late I've been giving attention to other matters. Apollo understands conditions at the barracoon, how much the cargo will bring on the Cuban market. I will send a message to him about your idea. He will have the message tonight."

"Do I give Apollo a bribe?"

"By all means. We could not trade without him. He's powerful in the city."

"It will have to be a small bribe," I said. "My funds are low."

"I'll make up the difference," Cicérone said. "I am glad to be rid of them."

He dabbed at his forehead with a lace-bordered handkerchief.

"The time is late," I said. "I have to return to my ship. Your foreman, Apollo, can I find him now at the barracoon?"

"I doubt it. He's a Houngan and tonight, this being a day of festival, you're apt to find him conducting voodoo rites."

"Where?"

"There are several places where the rites are held. Your driver will know."

"You'll send a message to Apollo in the morning early?"

"Tonight," Cicérone replied, and mumbled something as he turned away.

Armand did remember. His carriage was waiting outside the gate. Music drifted down from the terrace on a breeze that was heavy with the scent of jasmine.

It was a good idea, I thought, that I talk to Apollo as soon as I could, tonight, if possible. Time was short. Many things could happen to my plans if they were delayed by so much as an hour or two.

TWELVE

∾ *I asked Thiot* if he knew the foreman at the warehouse of Cicérone and Lynne.

"Henri Apollo?"

"Whatever his name is."

"Yes, Apollo. He is the foreman."

"Are you a friend?"

"Nobody is a friend of Apollo."

"Do you know him?"

"Yes, by eye."

"Would he be around tonight, anywhere?"

The driver thought for a moment, meanwhile flicking his whip at the bugs that were swarming about us.

"Apollo is the Houngan," he said. "The people meet on festive nights. Tonight, perhaps. Why do you ask?"

"I wish to talk."

We drove through the town toward the sea and

soon to the left came upon a byway massed with dark trees, upon a narrow lane where a lamp flickered beside a *tonnelle* whose door was painted with the figure of a coiled snake.

"I will bring him," Armand Thiot said. "Wait, my friend."

After a long time, he came back with a man of massive size, no longer young, with gray hair and a gray goatee.

Apollo said he could not talk now, since the ceremonies have begun. "But come with me," he said, "and we will talk later."

I followed him through the door with the painted snake into a room that was narrow and some thirty feet in length. It was already crowded. We took seats on a bench near the door, in the shadows.

Apollo stood at the far end of the room, in front of an altar that held thunder stones, polished and glistening black, the *asson* made of beads and the vertebrae of a snake. It held fruit, cakes of meal, ears of corn, cups, conches, and an egg, the ancient symbol of fertility and of life.

"Let us put ourselves in the presence of God," Apollo, the Houngan, intoned.

To the rattling of beads and the bones of the snake, the signs of the Cross blending with the signs of Voodoo, he recited the litany of the saints: Jacques, Peter, Nicolas, Joseph, Luc — followed by the *loas:*

68

Damballa, Wedo, Erzilie, Legba, Ogoun Ferreille . . .

The Houngan made the design on the floor with handfuls of meal, the black goat was brought forward covered with a red cloak, the flashing sword caught the light of the candles, and an attendant rushed in with a gourd to catch its blood.

Men and women began to move around, pausing to drink from a receptacle filled with water and herbs. The papa drum thundered. The mama drum joined him. The earth began to move to the tread of dancers.

The drums changed their rhythm. The anthem of the war god, Ogoun Ferreille, suddenly broke from every throat. The dancers crouched in froglike postures, their knees almost touching the floor. With green meal the Houngan drew another design in front of the altar. This time it was the emblem of the god. Drums thundered, calling him down, down, down . . .

The drums throbbed inside my skin, inside my very bones. I raised my hands above my head and stared beyond the *tonnelle*'s slanting roof, beyond the silent trees into the starry cave of heaven. I opened my hands. My fingers seemed on fire. I no longer breathed, but stood there in the swaying room, transfixed.

It was Thiot's voice that brought me back.

"Much noise," he said. "The drums, they depress the ears. Lots of noise. The rattle of the snake bones I like better."

The ceremony had ended. Thiot took me by the arm and we made our way to the carriage. We waited for a long time for Apollo to come. He was glistening with sweat and spoke to me in the tones he had used at the rites.

"What is it, M'seiur?" he said.

"Monsieur Cicérone tells me that you are the foreman at the barracoon."

"That is true."

"I'm a friend of Cicérone. My father, Mr. Lynne, is his partner. I will come to the warehouse tomorrow."

"For what reasons?"

"For reasons of business. I will come early. What time are you there?"

"I am always there. M'sieur Cicérone comes once a week, once a month, but Apollo is there always. Always except when I am not there, but here at the *tonnelle*."

"Is seven o'clock too early?"

"Seven o'clock is the hour I eat my breakfast. My first breakfast. I eat breakfasts all day. That is how I keep in good health and in the good graces of my patron, Mamballa."

"I will come then."

"At seven by the clock," the Houngan said. "But how does Apollo know that you are the gentleman you talk about? The *blancs* talk many things to Apollo. Some things are true and some are untrue. Apollo wishes to know the truth. The cat that is scalded is afraid of the cold water. You understand, no?"

"I understand," I answered, looking up at the massive Negro. "Monsieur Cicérone will send you a message. I have just talked to him."

"It is better that Apollo gets a message. Then everything will be clear in his head, yes."

"At seven in the morning," I replied.

"If Apollo gets no message, the door it will be closed."

"At seven," I repeated.

"Perhaps," Apollo answered. "Yes."

On the beach I found a fisherman dozing in his boat and paid him to row me back to the ship. I slept little that night, fearing that I would be late for my meeting with Henri Apollo.

Chapter ∾
THIRTEEN

∾*In the morning* I rowed myself ashore, leaving word for Chief Petty Officer Carroll that I would be back on the ship by noon and perhaps would have some passengers with me.

It was already hot. The bay was shimmering like hot brass. I found Henri Apollo sitting in his small office with his big bare feet propped up on a table, eating a melon-sized papaya without a spoon.

He was a bigger man than he had looked the night before, stronger and more youthful. Indeed, he was of mammoth proportions — one of the biggest men I have ever seen — the only one bigger being the strong man in a circus my brother had taken me to one time in New Orleans.

He looked up without speaking, his mouth full of papaya, and a far-off gaze in his red-rimmed eyes.

"I have been told that you will be taking cargo," he said. "M'sieur Cicérone told me."

Mingled with the fresh sweet scent of the papaya

Apollo was consuming, there was the strong odor of many bodies. From a distance I heard the murmur of voices and the cry of a child, again a part of a girl's song.

"How many?" I asked.

"They come in every day," Apollo said, spitting a black papaya seed on the floor. "Today there are two hundred and sixteen, not counting children and the babies. Tomorrow, who knows? Maybe three hundred. Maybe less."

Apollo sliced another papaya, using a small, curved bush knife that lay on his desk, and gave me half of it.

"Where do you go?" he asked.

"To Cuba."

"That is the best, Apollo thinks."

He sliced another papaya neatly in half with one tap of his brisk knife. "James Lynne. Lynne. Have you something to do with a Lynne who is a man I knew, who is a partner of M'sieur Cicérone?"

"I'm his son," I said, "as I have told you."

Apollo spat out a mouthful of seeds and wiped the blade of his bush knife across his broad thigh and thrust it in his belt. He rose to his feet and bowed.

"Glad to greet you, M'sieur Lynne. You come now to see the goods we have in the warehouse."

"I would like to see them."

We left the small room that smelled of sweet papayas and went into a long corridor lit by a single flare, where the stench of human bodies was heavy. On each side were bales of cotton and sacks of sugar. At the end of the corridor was a barred door. Through the bars I saw another room, which had no other door, and two barred windows, high up against the ceiling, too small even for a child to crawl through.

It was a room large enough for two families. It was full, so crammed with bodies that there was no place to lie, only to stand or crouch. The room was dark. Fortunately I could see no faces.

"When do they eat?" I asked.

"Any time now," Apollo said. "Curel brings his cart and he pushes it in. He'll be here soon. We have a good catch. We should make a basketful of reales with it. The last one was not worth a barrel of bad rum, all of them together. Most were sick and died on us before we got to Cuba. This catch comes from La Hotte. We have never had a cargo from La Hotte before."

I had heard of La Hotte. It was a place in the mountains where the people lived in scattered villages. They were poor but fiercely proud and lived in such seclusion that they seldom fell under the watchful eyes of the district authorities.

74

It was these authorities who were the key to slave-running in Haiti, in the time of my father and also in the time of his father.

The method was simple, to hear my brother tell it. Any breaking of a law, no matter how small, landed the culprit before a judge, who for a small fee turned him or her over to an official. For another small fee, the official passed him on directly to a slave catcher. These renegades then collected their cargo, going in carts from town to town, and delivered it at night to the warehouse of Cicérone and Lynne or to some other firm dealing in slaves.

"Curel comes now with his cart. You will see how healthy they are, what appetites they have."

I had seen and heard enough. My stomach was churning with the smells and the sounds. We went back to Apollo's office, passing Curel on the way, trundling his cart heaped with week-old fruit.

"They should bring a price," Apollo said. "The market is good now in Cuba."

I went to the window and looked out across the bay. The *Dauphine* rode gently on the brassy sea.

"Get your cargo together," I told Apollo. "Give them a chance to eat but have them on the dock not later than an hour from now with all their belongings, if they have any. Send Curel to the store and have him bring back a cartload of shovels and hoes, bush knives and axes. As many as he can carry, maybe thirty of each. Charge them to our account."

Apollo gave me a puzzled look. It was something he had never been asked to do before.

"Should we not wait for M'sieur Cicérone?"

"We should not wait for him or for anyone. As I said, I have already talked with Cicérone. We have a schedule that we cannot delay. The ship sails before noon. There's a war, remember?"

Apollo was still puzzled. He stood in the doorway, filling it with his huge frame. He looked like Henri Christophe, the mad emperor who had freed the slaves of Haiti, then killed twenty thousand by working them to death in the quarries or making them haul the stones along jungle trails for his great castle and fort, Sans Souci. The two men, from pictures I had seen of Henri Christophe, had the same look about them.

"You do not wish to wait for M'sieur Cicérone?" Apollo asked.

"No."

Apollo hitched up his broad belt, which was made of snakeskin. "This is a good cargo, M'sieur Lynne. Apollo should have extra money for so many good ones."

"You'll be paid," I said.

"Apollo should have the money now."

76

"I have no money with me. You can get it from Cicérone."

"Now is the best time."

He looked more than ever like the mad Henri Christophe. I pulled my jacket back in a casual movement that revealed the blue-burnished pistol at my hip.

Apollo pretended that he did not see it. "A little of the money now," he said, holding out his hand.

"Later. I've told you that I have no money. Later."

The massive Negro pointed toward the pistol hidden under my coat. "Apollo will take that. The one with the blue nose. Apollo likes that."

The Houngan towered above me. In a contest of strength he would break me in two like a dry stick. I unfastened the navy pistol from my hip — we had two more just like it in the ship's locker. I took out the cartridges and put the pistol in his outstretched hand.

I waited until he pushed it down between his boa belt and his bare skin.

"I'll be back in less than an hour," I said. "Have the cargo ready for me."

"Bring some of the silver," Apollo said.

When I reached the *Dauphine*, Carroll was waiting for me. With him was Lambert, a seaman.

"Don't tie her up," Carroll shouted, as he and Lambert came down the ladder.

"When will you be back?" I asked him.

"Maybe never," he answered.

He did not know how prophetic his words would prove to be.

Left aboard were Lem Wilson and Alex Colby, not much of a crew to get the *Dauphine* to the dock, load the ship, and sail it out of the harbor.

As we hauled in the anchor, which fortunately lay in shallow water and was not hard to free, Lem spoke.

"What are we doing, Jim?"

"Taking in the anchor."

"What for?"

"We're going to load two hundred Negro slaves and move them out of Port-au-Prince."

"Who said? Captain Semmes didn't say anything about moving slaves."

"No, but they belong to me, half of them, and I'm going to set them free."

"How're you going to do that?"

"The way Captain Semmes freed you. Something like it, anyway."

"That was different, him making me free."

"Not at all. It's the same."

Lem was still unconvinced. I called Alex over to

help out. It also took valuable time to half-convince him, but together the three of us finally horsed the *Dauphine* into the dock. We gave the piling a resounding bump as we did so, but managed to tie her up without further mishap.

Chapter ∽
FOURTEEN

∽*Apollo stood* at the main gate of the warehouse with a knife in his belt. Before I left the ship I had filled a pocket with silver coins and two of gold, confiscated from the *Dauphine.* I walked up to him, and seeing that he meant to block my path, dumped the coins in his outstretched paws. He bowed and led me inside.

My navy pistol lay on a table among the rinds of the papayas he had been eating. He now picked it up and thrust it in his snakeskin belt beside the knife.

"Have you had a message from Ruiz Cicérone?" I said.

"The message it came a long time ago this morning while Apollo was asleep, yes."

"The cargo's ready?"

"She is ready, like M'sieur Cicérone commanded. He will come later when the sun is high up, he."

I had no intention of waiting until Cicérone came. "We'll start loading the cargo now," I said.

Apollo reached out, took a piece of papaya from the table, and thrust it into his mouth. He chewed the fruit and slowly swallowed, and spat two black seeds upon the littered floor. He hitched up his belt. He then filled his enormous chest with one long breath and motioned me to follow him.

The long corridor was filled with blacks, a long line that disappeared in the gloom. From far at the end of the corridor I heard the voices of two guards shouting for the line to move. A pistol went off, two shots in quick succession. The sounds echoed and died away. The line began to move.

With Apollo on one side, a guard on the other, and two guards at the rear, the blacks moved silently on their bare feet across the dock and up the gangplank. I had stationed Lem Wilson at the head of the plank. Between us we separated the men from the women and children. The men I headed below to the cargo hold; the women I kept on deck for the time being.

During all of this Apollo said nothing, but from time to time I saw him glance toward the Champs de Mars. I still had no thought of waiting for Monsieur Cicérone.

"We'll move the ship away from the dock," I told him, "just in case someone happens by."

"Apollo, he says that is wise. Mostly we fill the ship at night when only the cats are prowling. That is the best time for loading the ship." He put his hand on the butt of the pistol. "You will wait for M'sieur Cicérone, yes?"

"We will wait," I said, pointing to the bay that already was shimmering in the hot sun.

The engine was running as Alex untied the lines and leaped aboard. I eased the ship into the bay. There, with room for the ship to drift, Lem and I went below, taking two lanterns. The blacks were crouching in the darkness. The lanterns shone on their faces and sweating bodies. Already there was little air in the hold and what there was smelled of fear.

I introduced myself by name, using French. "The captain has deserted the ship," I said. "Having been second in command, I now take his place as captain."

More than a hundred men crouched there in the darkness, but the hold could have been empty, for all the sounds that came to me.

"You are here because of misfortune. I inform you that you are again free men. I ask your advice in a matter that concerns us all. If you choose, I will take you to Cuba. What fortune would await you there I don't know. I can return you to Haiti, let you ashore some place on the far side, where you could

82

find your way home. Or I can put you ashore on a secluded island a day's hard sailing from here, called Encantadora, 'Enchantress.' I have brought hoes and other utensils that will be needed for planting. You know the risks better than I. It is up to you to decide. I will come back shortly. Tell me then what you wish to do."

There was a suspicious silence as I left, but when I returned the hold was a bedlam of voices. I lifted my lantern. Quiet settled over the crowd. Someone stood up far to the rear. I could not see his face, but when he spoke I judged him to be a young man.

"We have decided," he said, speaking in French mixed with a word or two of Haitian, "that we might like to go to the island you told about. What do you know of this island?"

"Nothing, except that when we passed it a few days ago and stopped to fill our casks with water, I was struck by the sight of a lush grove of coconuts, bananas, and other fruits. I also saw a sheltered bay with a stream running into it. We passed the full length of the island, which measures about ten miles on the chart, and saw no one. Nor the smoke from any fire."

A shout went up, which I took to be a sign of agreement. When the din faded away the man came forward. He was, as I had thought, not much older than I and, as I learned later, the son of a native chieftain. His name was Lumando and his presence was commanding.

"We have chosen to go to the island you speak of," he said.

"Then let's go at once," I answered.

Through Lumando's efforts, I recruited twelve prospective sailors, divided them into four watches, and taught them some of the rudiments of handling sails. We did not try to spread all our canvas but were content with driving and steadying sail forward.

With the help of our rusty engine we arrived at Encantadora the next afternoon. For an hour it had been raining, but as we made our turn into the crescent-shaped bay, the rain ceased and the sun broke through, pouring a dazzling sheen across shore and jungle.

We stayed aboard that night and in the morning at daylight began to ferry the crowd ashore in our longboats, ten at a time, along with armloads of axes, shovels, hoes, and bush knives. The *Dauphine* was well stocked with sealed tins of butter, barrels of salt pork and beef, and a hogshead of salt. And these we carried ashore also.

The island looked as if it teemed with game and around the ship schools of fish were swimming, even turtles, larger than any I had ever seen.

I let Lumando know by my chart that the island was off the beaten track, that with any luck he could live there for his lifetime and never see another ship.

The island seemed to be solid jungle made up of several different kinds of trees, many of them bearing fruit. Where these trees grew, so would berries, edible roots, and yams. The people had tools to fell the forest and till the soil. They had a plentiful supply of running water. The supplies from the ship would tide them over until they could grow a crop of melons, whose dried husks I saw along the shore and the edge of the jungle.

There was no need for me to warn Lumando to build his village inland, away from the shore. People who had lived their lives in daily fear would take this precaution.

We left them one of our longboats and did not tarry, being late already. We shook hands all around, which consumed some time but seemed to give everyone confidence that we were not playing a trick on them.

We left the more than two hundred people on the shore, waving at us and cheering, but still, I am certain, unbelieving.

With a following wind we set all sail and headed for Cienfuegos, where we lay around for three days.

Alex Colby began to feel uncomfortable.

"You know," he said to me, "we could be tried for deserters."

"Tried and hung by our necks," Lem broke in.

"Maybe we should stay here or head back to Haiti and wait out the war," Alex went on.

"I'm for going on to Fayal, as Captain Semmes instructed us to do," I said.

"I'll take a chance and stay here," Alex announced after some thought.

"How about you?" I asked Lem.

"I'm ready to go find the captain," Lem said.

I felt the same love for Captain Semmes that Lem Wilson did. And for the land of my birth, though the thought of slavery and my father's part in it troubled me greatly. But strong as both of these was my love for the *290*. Willingly I would have set off across the Atlantic Ocean in one of the *Dauphine*'s leaky lifeboats, if necessary, to find her.

At the last minute Alex decided to go with us and by luck we picked up six experienced sailors at the waterfront, one of them a former ship's mate. We put aboard enough food for three weeks and set off for Fayal in the Azores, giving the northeastern part of Cuba, which was alive with Yankee warships, a wide berth.

Still flying the French flag, to deceive any Yankees that might be about, we made our landfall in good time. We stayed clear of the Yankee whaling ships that had begun to arrive at the islands. But we had a long wait for Semmes and the *290*. She passed Fayal late in May. Only by chance did she sight us as we lay at anchor.

She was no longer the trim fighting ship she had been. Between the time we had left her in Cuban waters, Captain Semmes had rounded the Cape of Good Hope twice, threaded the straits between Java and Sumatra, and sailed as far east as Singapore. The ship was tired, the crew was tired, and he was tired.

We transferred our few belongings. Lem took along the French flag and the chronometer, which pleased Captain Semmes. He was not pleased, however, at our failure to meet him in Cuban waters and our long absence.

No sooner had I gone aboard the *290*, than he sent word for me to appear. I found him in his cabin working on the ship's log. He put aside his pen, looked me up and down, and then picking up his pen, began to write in the logbook.

"We missed you in Cuban waters," he said, his pen skipping over the page. "We waited five days, days we could ill afford to waste."

He paused and glanced up at me. His hair was grayer than I remembered and there was gray in his mustache, but the fire had not gone out of his gaze.

I told him the truth, everything that had taken place. I told him about my father, my talk with Ruiz Cicérone, my encounter with Apollo, and how I had emptied the barracoon and settled the slaves on Encantadora Island.

"A bit high-handed," he said. "Playing God, don't you think? The slaves weren't yours. They belonged to your father and his partner. And how do you know that the people you set down upon a strange island will prosper there? As a matter of fact, how do you know that they will even survive?"

It *was* high-handed of me, I now realized, but I did not apologize. I stood upon what I had done. I didn't care whether the men and women and children belonged to Cicérone and Lynne or not. Nor did I fear that they would not survive on the island. They were better off there than in the barracoon or on someone's plantation, I decided.

I was silent. Captain Semmes was once more writing in his logbook. He seemed to have forgotten me. There were no sounds except the scratching of his pen and a noise from the deck above.

Captain Semmes paused. "Do you hear a scraping on the deck?"

"Yes, sir."

"Do you know what it is?"

"It's the sound of a holystone."

"So it is. Will you be so kind as to go on deck and take the stone from the man who is using it and use it on the deck? Use it the rest of the morning and every morning for the next week."

"Yes, sir, thank you, sir," I said.

"You are welcome," replied Captain Semmes.

As I reached the door Captain Semmes had an afterthought. "And when not scraping the deck," he said, "you will be confined to your quarters for a period of seven days."

"Yes, sir," I said, thankful that he was in a good frame of mind, and my punishment was no worse.

At noon of that day we put the *Dauphine* to the torch. She made a fine fire. While she was still burning, we set a straight course for the English Channel and Cherbourg. The French port of Cherbourg was in neutral country, the closest port where we could refit our sea-worn ship. It proved to be a fateful voyage.

Chapter ∿
FIFTEEN

∿ *The arrival* of the 290 at Cherbourg was unexpected. For more than four months her location had gone unreported both in Europe and in America. No word had come from Capetown of the two ships she had sunk nearby, or of the thirty-seven passengers she now carried. She was a ghost ship.

Some of this information I got from Lieutenant Kell the first day after Captain Semmes hailed us at Fayal.

He was on duty in the engine room. He looked pinched and his skin was the color of mahogany from the tropic sun.

"The ship's a wreck," he told me. "Her magazines are filled with inferior powder. I think it was made in somebody's backyard. Her seams are all in bad need of caulking. There's rust in many places where it shouldn't be."

"She's still moving," I said. "And she looks spry

under sail. I remember when she first came upon us. She looked as if she'd just been launched."

"That's because you were glad to see her."

"It was the gladdest moment of my life, when she loomed out of the mist," I said. "A week's rest should put her back in shape again," I added glibly.

"More than a week, lad. She'll need all of two months. She's a weary ship, and make no mistake. The men are exhausted. We need a long rest."

The 290 was no longer a ghost ship, whose whereabouts was unknown, as she sailed out of the Channel mist and anchored off the French naval dock. News of her arrival was flashed by telegraph to every capital on the continent. The people of Cherbourg came rushing out of their houses to see her. But then a more important thing happened.

The news reached Flushing, Holland, where the Federal cruiser *Kearsarge* lay moored on the Scheldt River. Three days later she was off Cherbourg.

Semmes knew the *Kearsarge* was coming. It is possible that he could have slipped out of the harbor and disappeared, as he had before from other harbors. But moved by a sense of pride and knowledge of the ship's poor condition, he chose to remain. In this gesture of defiance our crew supported him. While we watched the *Kearsarge* sail into Cherbourg, we anxiously awaited the word that would send us into battle. There was not one among us who wished to flee the harbor. Everyone, to a man, stood solidly behind Captain Semmes.

In midafternoon, her officers and crew craning their necks at the rail, the *Kearsarge* steamed within pointblank range of the 290, and observed her in detail from stem to stern. She then ran out beyond the breakwater to loiter there between Pointe de Querqueville and Isle Pelée, with the obvious purpose of preventing our escape. She did not know that Captain Semmes intended to stay and fight.

But she knew it soon, indeed by message, shortly after she had cruised menacingly by us in a gesture that could be taken in no other way than as a challenge. The message was sent to the Confederate agent at Cherbourg, who was requested to relay it to Captain John Winslow of the *Kearsarge*. It read:

> Sir: I hear that you were informed by the U.S. Consul that the *Kearsarge* was to come to this port solely for the prisoners landed by me, and that she was to depart in twenty-four hours. I desire to say to the U.S. Consul that my intention is to fight the *Kearsarge* as soon as I can make the necessary arrangements. I hope these will not detain me more than until tomorrow evening, or after the morrow morning at the furthest. I beg she will not depart before I am ready to get out.

92

I have the honor to be, very respectfully,
your obedient servant,

R. Semmes, Captain

The message reached Captain Winslow that night.
The next morning, with battle now a certainty, our
glasses were trained on the *Kearsarge*, who in turn
fixed her glasses upon us.

She was a modern steam sloop, not as maneuver-
able as the *290*, but mounting two 11-inch Dahlgrens,
which gave her a heavier broadside. She was strictly
a man-of-war, staunch and built to fight, while our
ship in comparison was designed for speed and agility — qualities that unfortunately we no longer pos-
sessed.

There was also a difference, it developed, in the
sizes of the two crews, our ship carrying 149 men,
the *Kearsarge* 163. And in the matter of marks-
manship they could be expected to be superior, since
our powder was low and poor in quality.

Her big advantage, however, was something of
which we were not aware that morning. It was a detail of construction that had gone unnoticed the pre-
vious afternoon when she steamed by us.

Though built of wood and so described in all the
reports of her in our possession, the *Kearsarge* during
the last year had been secretly armored. On both
sides of her vulnerable midsection, protecting her

boilers, were one hundred twenty fathoms of sheet chain, bolted to the hull, boxed and concealed by one-inch oak planking.

Captain Semmes in his message to Captain Winslow had indicated that he would be ready to fight on Thursday, specifically on the sixteenth of June, 1864, but preparations took longer than expected.

French authorities at first refused to coal our ship, then canceled the order and filled the bunkers to capacity. Light spars and top hamper were removed, the decks holystoned, the brass polished. Gun crews cleaned the batteries, arranged relays of shot, shell, and powder from the magazines. Pikes and cutlasses were brought on deck, boarding tactics rehearsed.

It was Saturday before the ship was ready.

That morning Captain Semmes sent ashore his treasure chest containing the ship's funds, and the chronometers taken from every prize he had captured.

That evening he granted the crew five hours' liberty, cautioning them to conduct themselves with pride for their ship and to return early. When the men had gone he followed them ashore and walked up the hill to a church, where he attended Mass and prayed.

Sunday morning dawned clear with a westerly wind and smooth seas. Before breakfast, orders were given to light the fires in the furnaces. Communication with the shore was then cut, sailors took their posts, the officers made a quick inspection, and the anchor slowly came up.

Standing nearby was the French warship *La Couronne,* which fell in behind us as we steamed out of the harbor. An English yacht, the *Deerhound,* with a John Lancaster and his family aboard, preceded us and took up a position beyond the breakwater from which they could watch the action.

The heights above Cherbourg were crowded with spectators, as were the mole, the shore, the fortifications and the upper stories of houses that commanded a view of the sea. From Paris had come a trainload of boulevardiers, sports enthusiasts and fashionable ladies, bringing with them box lunches and campstools.

The French warship anchored at the three-mile limit, and we could see the *Kearsarge* moving away from us in an obvious effort to draw us farther offshore, at a distance from which we would be unable to reach the protection of the harbor should the battle turn against us.

The boatswain and his mates piped all hands aft. Mounting a gun carriage, elegant in his gray uniform, pale but calm, Captain Semmes in a clear voice addressed the crew:

Officers and seamen of the *Alabama!* You have, at length, another opportunity of meeting the enemy — the first that has been presented to you since you sank the *Hatteras.* In the meantime, you have been all over the world, and it is not too much to say that you have destroyed, and driven for protection under neutral flags, one half of the enemy's commerce, which, at the beginning of the war, covered every sea. This is an achievement of which you may well be proud, and a grateful country will not be unmindful of it.

"The name of your ship," the Captain went on, "has become a household word wherever civilization extends. Shall that name be tarnished in defeat?"

Cries of "Never! Never!" answered him. Lem Wilson shouted louder than the rest of the crew. But I remained silent, seized suddenly by wonder that I was about to go into battle.

"The thing is impossible," Semmes continued. "Remember that you are in the English Channel, the theater of so much of the naval glory of our race, and that the eyes of all Europe are at this moment upon you. The flag that floats over you is that of a young Republic, who bids defiance to her enemies, whenever and wherever found."

Our crew cheered again and recovering from my silence I joined them. Lem Wilson, who stood be-

96

side me at the rail, gave out a piercing whistle. Then
we both raised our fists against the *Kearsarge*, which
was still moving away in an effort to draw us after
her.

"How do you feel, Jim?" Lem said.

"Good! And you?"

"Like fighting. We'll sink the Yank ship with our
first shot."

"Or the second."

Captain Semmes took his station on the horseblock
abreast the mizzenmast. He had lost weight and his
gray uniform looked too big for him. His face was
pale in the morning light. But as his voice rang out
across the deck it had fire in it.

"Go to your quarters!" he shouted.

Chapter ∾
SIXTEEN

∾ *It was now clear* that the *Kearsarge* would hold
to her position and that our approach would be north
by west.

A 32-pounder was therefore shifted from port to
starboard, thus creating a broadside of four guns.
The change in weight caused the ship to list to starboard by some two feet, which exposed less of our
surface to enemy fire.

The officers were attired in dress uniforms, the
crew in their freshest and best, except the gunners,
who were stripped to the waist, as were Lem Wilson
and myself, stationed in the engine room.

Less than an hour after the *290* passed the breakwater, the two ships stood at a distance from each
other of about a mile and a quarter. We were seven
miles northeast of Cherbourg when I was sent on
deck to report the action.

Suddenly the *Kearsarge* wheeled and steered a
head-on course toward the *290* in an effort to ram and

sink us or, failing this, to engage us at close quarters, or pass astern and rake us.

It was 10:57, the sea still calm, and both ships were under steam alone. Semmes, at the mizzen-mast, turned to Lieutenant Kell.

"Are you ready, Mr. Kell?" he asked.

"Aye, aye, sir. Ready and willing."

"Then you may open fire at once, sir."

At twelve hundred yards the *290* began the action with a 100-pound shell, followed by a salvo from her entire starboard battery. Unharmed, the *Kearsarge* took three broadsides before she deigned to answer. Her shots fell short.

Under a full head of steam, the *Kearsarge* did not alter her course, and to counter this move Semmes sheered to port. The enemy matched our change, bringing the ships closer together. They then began to pursue each other, in a series of diminishing cir-cles, each presenting her starboard broadside as she passed.

At first we fired two shots for every one we re-ceived, but our aim was high, and it was a quarter of an hour before we sent a 100-pound shell into the enemy's sternpost. The *Kearsarge* buckled under the blow, and I counted the seconds as I waited for the explosion that would destroy her rudder. It did not come.

I dove down the ladder to relay the information. All the men in the engine room stopped work to listen. A minute passed and there was no sound. A second minute passed. A third. We waited. Defective, as we learned later, the shell failed to burst. Had it done so the *Kearsarge* would have been put out of action. We would have sailed rings around her, raking the rudderless ship from every angle.

Now we were getting instructions from the speaking tube and every few minutes Lem Wilson, who had been sent on deck, would clamber down the ladder with word from Lieutenant Kell.

I was kept in the engine room and told to shovel coal as if my life depended upon it. And it did. I helped to keep the gauges high, so high that the boilers were ready to fly apart.

Firing from our ship grew steadier as we moved clockwise in circles, trending, it seemed, to the west. Lem came down the ladder to call me above to help service one of the 32-pounders.

As I took up my station a Blakely shell caved in the *Kearsarge*'s starboard bulwark and exploded on the quarter-deck. Two shots passed through open gun ports and another set her hammock netting afire. It became apparent, however, that we had not only a number of defective shells and weak powder, but also that all the hits scored against the enemy's sides had fallen harmlessly into the water.

100

Captain Semmes changed to solid shot, but these, too, were deflected by the *Kearsarge*'s concealed armor, of which we were still unaware.

Meanwhile the enemy had found the range with her 11-inch Dahlgrens. One of these shells crashed through a port just as the loaded gun was run out to fire. Ship's coxswain Michael Mars, acting as compressor man, was on his knees ready to dampen the recoil. The shell killed or wounded every seaman on one side of the piece, except Alex Colby. He waved me to his side and, working together, we shoveled the dead overboard and cleared the carnage as best we could.

The *290*'s gaff was then shot away, the ensign fell, and was replaced at the mizzenmasthead.

Suddenly a shell struck a gun carriage not more than five paces from where I stood. By right good fortune it did not explode. But it did careen crazily against a barrel of sand which thereupon upset, knocking me to the deck.

I got to my feet and stood stunned for a while. The live shell was still careening around on the slippery deck when I came to. It banged against the rail, rebounded, and as if it had eyes, slid between four men of a gun crew without touching one of them.

The shell made another dive toward me. I avoided it by jumping in the air. It slid under me and banged against a bulwark. I set off in pursuit as the shell headed forward along the deck. I overtook it at the moment it struck a hatch cover.

The heavy shell was like a greased pig. I picked it up and dropped it. Then I picked it up again and staggered to the rail, where with what strength was left to me, I dropped it, still unexploded, into the sea.

Forthwith I fell to the deck and sat there in a heap collecting my wits, while guns belched fire around me. Not until I got back on my feet did I see that my right hand was bleeding and that somehow I had crushed three of my fingers.

A fourth shell struck the hull at the waterline. A fragment struck Captain Semmes's right arm and, beckoning to a quartermaster, he stood on the horseblock directing the action while the blood was staunched.

The ship was now responding slowly to the helm, and Semmes sent Lieutenant Kell below to demand more steam.

Second Assistant Engineer William Brooks told Kell, "We have every inch of steam safe to carry without being blown up!"

Lieutenant Kell shouted, "Let her have steam! We had better blow her to hell than let the Yankees whip us."

We were completing the last of the seven circles. The two ships were now less than five hundred yards apart. In the hope of making the French coast before the ship sank, Captain Semmes put on all sail.

The 290 was still sluggish and Alex Colby was ordered to loosen the jib. The command was executed and Colby was returning when a shell struck him, inflicting a desperate wound. He clung to the jib boom and worked his way along a footrope to the deck. Here, beating his head with his arms, he fell to the deck dead.

Our ship was fast settling in the water. Her guns, those that were left, were firing sporadically. Semmes sent Kell below to estimate the time the ship could stay afloat.

All the compartments were crushed into one. The surgeon's operating table had received a direct hit. Kell returned to say that the ship could not last another ten minutes.

"Then, sir, cease firing," Semmes said. "Shorten sail and haul the colors."

The flag came down, but the *Kearsarge* kept up her fire. She fired five times into the sinking 290.

Lieutenant Kell, at an order from Semmes, shouted, "Every man save himself who can!"

Most of our boats had been smashed. As the ship began to sink, I heaved a grating overboard and jumped in after it. The *Deerhound* and French luggers from Cherbourg were making for us. The water was freezing cold.

I stared blankly at the angry water, the spinning pool she left behind. It was a horrible sight to me, this death of a beautiful ship. I tried to put the scene out of my mind as I swam away through the wreckage-strewn waves, but a part of me had gone down with the ship.

I found myself not more than fifty feet from Lem Wilson. In one hand he held a sack full of something. With the other he grasped a half-length of the ship's timber. With all my strength I clung to the wood grating. He was shouting to me but I didn't have enough breath to answer.

Chapter

SEVENTEEN

⌒ *My last memory* of the ship, as I left her splintered and bloody deck, was of Captain Semmes and Lieutenant Kell standing erect at the rail. Near them wisps of smoke and steam trickled from the stack. For a while they stood side by side, gazing at the *Kearsarge*. Then, unbuckling their swords, they hurled them into the sea.

How gallant Captain Semmes looked as he stood there at the ship's rail and faced the *Kearsarge*! The long voyage, during which he had sunk more than eighty enemy ships, had come to an end, but he remained, as his sword sank beneath the waves, defiant as ever.

I assumed that the two men had jumped overboard, but I could not find them now among the drifting mass of wreckage and bobbing heads the *290* left behind her.

A small raft of shell boxes floated past. Sprawled

upon it was Surgeon Llewellyn, lying face downward. He was dead. A dozen yards from me a sailor whose blackened face I couldn't recognize sank before I reached him. Another sailor nearby, crying for help, vanished as I came within arm's length.

Lem Wilson floated closer.

"That crate's about to sink you," I shouted.

"It's got valuables," he answered.

"Drop it," I shouted back. "We're half a mile from shore yet."

"I've been carting it for a long time," he said, still hanging on to the crate as if it were a bag of bullion.

"What is it?" I said as we drifted together.

"Says *Valuables*, Jim. That's all I know. Valuables."

At this moment a box floated by, half in the water, half out. In red paint, like that on Lem's crate, it also said *Valuables*. I reached out and pulled it to me, heading for shore, clinging to the box and the water-logged grating. They were not the dark canoe that saved Ishmael, but they kept me afloat.

I saw the *Deerhound* drift over the spot where the *290* had sunk. Two of her boats were in the water and had begun to pick up survivors, tossing ropes to some, hauling others over the sides.

Beyond her I saw the *Kearsarge* nosing in at last, beginning to lower her quarter-boats. I suddenly realized that if I were picked up by the warship I would forthwith become a Federal prisoner.

The *Deerhound*'s boats were a hundred yards from Lem and me, the others at nearly twice that distance.

Kicking off my boots, I abandoned the grating but clung to the box. The cold water had already stiffened my arms and choppy waves broke over my head, so I found it difficult to see or make out directions. I truthfully think that I would have drowned only six strokes from one of the *Deerhound*'s boats had one of her seaman not thrown me a line.

The quarter-boat was deeply laden with the officers and men of the *290*, the wounded, the half-drowned, some moaning, some deathly quiet. Prone on the sternsheets lay Captain Semmes, white-faced and unmoving, the bandage torn from his arm, but alive. Lieutenant Kell, disguised by a seaman's hat with the name *Deerhound* on it, had taken up an oar and stood watching as one of the *Kearsarge*'s boats came within hailing distance.

A blue-clad officer shouted, "Have you seen Captain Semmes?"

"Captain Semmes has drowned," Kell shouted back.

"Proceed to the *Kearsarge*," came the command.

Kell did not reply. Semmes lay quiet in the sternsheets.

Another seaman was dragged aboard, the crew bent to the sweeps and, ordered by Kell not to approach the *Kearsarge*, swept by it in a wide arc toward the *Deerhound*.

The yacht's second boat had already unloaded and we first lifted Captain Semmes up the ladder and then the wounded. We had no way of knowing how many of our officers and crew had been left behind, how many the enemy had gathered up.

There now were twenty-seven of our men, including Lem and me, aboard the *Deerhound*, eleven petty officers, Lieutenants Kell, Sinclair, and Howell, Captain Semmes, Lem, and I. (Sinclair, first pulled out of the water by one of the *Kearsarge*'s boats, slipped over the side and swam to the yacht.)

We presented John Lancaster, owner of the *Deerhound*, with a problem.

"I think every man has been picked up," he told Semmes. "Where shall I land you?"

Semmes replied, "I am now under English colors and the sooner you put me, with my officers and men, on English soil, the better."

The *Kearsarge* was lying not more than half a mile away and it was apparent that Captain Winslow expected the *Deerhound* to deliver all the survivors to him. But Lancaster, a man of mettle, raised anchor and steamed into the Channel.

As we passed the *Kearsarge* we could see gunners at their posts and general activity on deck. We learned after we reached England that Winslow's officers had pled with him to fire on us, but aware that he would be attacking a ship flying British colors, he resisted the temptation.

The owner of the *Deerhound* found comfortable quarters for those who had survived. He also had a fine chef aboard and we fared well, better than on the 290. The evening we arrived in England he made us a surprise treat — a special French cake with a dozen eggs in it and a lot of fancy icing on top.

Captain Semmes recovered quickly from his wound, but was quiet, grieving for his lost ship. We all grieved. As for my hand, it was swollen twice its usual size and pained me greatly.

News of the battle had preceded us and we were warmly greeted by citizens of the port, among them Confederate officials, who offered Captain Semmes a fresh ship. This offer, which was merely a gesture since there was no ship available, he refused out of weariness and depression.

The crew was paid off from the gold Semmes had sent ashore at Cherbourg. Lem and I got less than the others and there was no prize money to distribute, none of the million dollars and more that each sailor had dreamed of sharing.

The *290* lay in forty fathoms of water. The battle, in which nine of our men were killed, twelve drowned, and twenty-two wounded, was over. It had been decided early by the shell that had struck the *Kearsarge's* sternpost and failed to go off.

The small number of those drowned was due to chance. Those on the *Deerhound* had debated before the fight whether to watch or not. They had even taken a vote, which resulted in a tie. The tie had been finally resolved by the vote of the youngest child, Catherine, aged nine. Such are two of fate's many faces!

As for the crates Lem and I found floating, mine turned out to be the more valuable. Lem's crate held a dozen porcelain dishes and a few teacups. But in mine was a silver tea set.

"What are you going to do with yours?" I asked Lem.

"Trade it for a bottle of rum."

"You should get two bottles."

"I'll ask for three. What are you going to do with the tea set?"

"Drink tea," I said. "There's a lot of it in England."

"What else, when you're not drinking tea?"

"I'm going back to Laird's and try to get my job again. I'll try to get you one, too."

110

Lem said, "You're not going home and fight for the South?"

I glanced at my bandaged hand. "I wouldn't be much good, Lem. But how about you?"

"I'd like to go back. Maybe not right now. But sometime when Captain Semmes finds another ship."

"He'll find one all right, but she won't be the *290*."

"If she isn't, what then?"

"I'd go with Semmes if he was captain of a barge," I said.

"Me too, Jim."

Chapter ~
EIGHTEEN

~At *Laird's* *shipyard* things had changed, as I
learned two days after I got to Liverpool.

It was a cold morning with a biting wind blowing
up the Mersey when I went in to see Mr. Bromley.
His office was warm with a bright fire burning in the
grate and Mr. Bromley himself standing at his big
drawing board smoking his long-stemmed pipe.

He came over and we shook hands. "You're looking healthier than when I left you on the Mersey," he
said, "as if you'd never been in a battle. But that's
the way with youth. It recovers quickly from misfortune."

I had brought along the silver tea set, wrapped in a
cloth bundle, and I handed it to Mr. Bromley. "For
your wife," I said.

He put it down on his drawing board, cut the
strings that bound it, and pulled out a shining
pitcher. I had spent my idle time coming home on

the *Deerhound* polishing it. It shone like new, as if it had never been in battle or afloat in Cherbourg Harbor.

While Mr. Bromley was admiring the pitcher, turning it to the firelight, turning it up to look on the bottom for the hallmark, I noticed that a young man stood at the drawing board that formerly had been mine. Another young man stood near him.

Mr. Bromley set the pitcher down and pulled out the sugar bowl, also gleaming like new. Of a sudden it occurred to me that Mr. Bromley might think that the silverware was a bribe.

"It's for your wife," I said. "I know she likes silver, because last Christmas you bought her a flower bowl."

"She does," said Mr. Bromley. "She'll swoon with delight. I can't thank you enough. I . . ."

"Besides bringing the silver, I came to see about my job," I said, giving the new young man a glance as I did so.

Mr. Bromley put the silver aside, sent the young man who had taken my place on an errand, and sat down on his three-legged stool.

My hand was still swollen. Mr. Bromley glanced at it. He wanted to know what happened and I told him.

"There's plenty of work, Jim. Semmes destroyed

113

more than half of the North's shipping. Orders for new ships are coming in faster than we can handle them. How long do you think it will take to heal?"

"I don't know. Maybe two weeks or longer."

I didn't tell him that I had gone to a surgeon as soon as I reached Liverpool, that the surgeon had told me I was lucky not to have lost all of my fingers, that three of them would always be stiff. They were, unfortunately, the fingers I held my pen with.

"There isn't any room here in the office now," Mr. Bromley said, shaking his head. "But I can find you a job in the yard. At something where you won't need to use your hand."

"I'd also like to find a job for a shipmate of mine, Lem Wilson," I said.

"No difficulty, Jim. Both of you come back tomorrow morning and I'll see that you go to work. It won't be what you're used to in the way of wages, but it will tide you over until your hand gets well."

"What if my hand doesn't get well?"

Mr. Bromley puffed on his pipe. "We'll wait and see. We'll solve that problem if the time comes."

He shook my good hand and patted me on the back. I think he was glad that I had come home.

"I want to hear about all your exploits," he said as we parted. "I would like to have been with you, Jim."

I said nothing more to Mr. Bromley, but I returned next morning. I brought Lem Wilson with me, since he was without a job. Mr. Bromley put us to work at once. We sat in a shack with a scale and weighed all the rivets that went into the various hulls Laird's was building. I put the rivets on the scale and told Lem what they weighed. He put the figures down in a work ledger. Every night I helped Lem tote up the weights.

Shortly after I began my new job, my brother stopped me as I was going out the gate at the noon hour. He looked seedy and down on his luck. He no longer carried the gold-headed cane. But his face lit up as he grasped my hand. He stepped back to survey me. There was a glint of a tear in his eyes.

"I heard you were here," he said. "I came down from London just to see you. My word, but you've changed." He paused suddenly and looked me over, just then becoming aware that I was dressed in workingman's clothes. "You have a new job?"

I nodded. "If you can call it that."

A shadow crossed his face. The cause was soon revealed, while we were drinking mugs of ale in the Mermaid's Grotto.

"I'm back in my rent," he said. "They're going to throw me into the street unless I pay up by tomorrow."

"I cashed my first week's pay yesterday. You can have half."

I dug down in my pocket and passed him the money, a meager sum.

"That's very generous of you," my brother said. He began to count. "One pound. One pound six. They don't pay you much, do they?"

"It's not much of a job," I replied. "Do you hear anything from Father?"

"Nothing. I told you about our falling out and that he'd cut me off in his will. I wrote him an apology when I cooled down. He never answered my letter. I guess our quarrel is permanent."

I told Ted about the 290 and what had happened to me in Port-au-Prince, how I had emptied the barracoon and how the Negroes had chosen to settle on Encantadora Island. In a way he had been responsible for my concern for the slaves, but it was clear to me he had never had one himself. North, South, slavery or no, none of it mattered to Ted.

"We might go into the business, Jim. Settle two or three of these islands, put the slaves to work growing sugar cane. We could buy beads and trinkets for the ladies and clothes and sandals for the men and barter the goods for sugar. Sugar's always in good demand. We'd make a mint."

Ted had grown rich on sugar by the time the whis-

116

tle at Laird's ended the noon hour. He was so boyish about his scheme that I had to smile. Of a sudden I felt like his older brother. For the first time in my life, as we shook hands and parted, I felt affection for him. I was never to see or hear from Ted again.

Through the summer I worked at Laird's, weighing iron plates and rivets, putting weights down in my ledger. Then late in September I received a letter from a barrister in New Orleans. It gently broke the news that my father had died in August and that, as the heir to his estate, I was asked to write immediately and say whether or not it was possible for me to come to New Orleans.

I sat down at once, answered the letter and mailed it. The next morning I took a ship for London, arriving at the India docks two days later. This was a Wednesday, the 29th day of September, 1864. One day later, Thursday afternoon, I hired on in the engine room of a steamer bound for New York.

Lem Wilson hired on with me. We sped down the Thames on the evening tide, past Deptford and Gravesend. A night wind came up, but the skies were clear and a quarter moon rode high in the east.

Whenever were we to land on American shores? By what roundabout way were we to reach New Orleans? In the war that still raged, what would be my role? How many months, even years, would pass before I found my way to Port-au-Prince?

There were no answers to these questions, or no surmises, at least none came to me. I was as confused as I was the moment they plucked me from the cold waters of Cherbourg bay or even the day I had signed on the 290. But I didn't search for the answers. Perhaps I had gained some confidence in my ability to meet things as they came and a belief that surprise was a part of life best not anticipated. It was enough now that I was on a ship once more, headed for the open sea.